a novel

By Roger Quam

Copyright © 2015 by Roger Quam

*The Garden*
by Roger Quam

Printed in the United States of America.

ISBN 9781498444088

All rights reserved solely by the author. The author guarantees all contents are original and do not infringe upon the legal rights of any other person or work. No part of this book may be reproduced in any form without the permission of the author. The views expressed in this book are not necessarily those of the publisher.

Unless otherwise indicated, Bible quotations are taken from the New King James Version. Copyright © 1982 by Thomas Nelson, Inc. Used by permission.

www.xulonpress.com

# Chapter 1

David was in a tight spot once again. His work for the Agency in the first year of his intelligence career sometimes made him wish that he had chosen some other vocation. He always knew he could depend on some God provided miracle to keep him from getting seriously injured, maimed, or even killed outright. He had been in tight situations before which would cause him to wonder if his time on earth may soon be up and he would go to meet his Maker. This time the predicament seemed overwhelming.

He was in Florida and involved with a drug case as a counter intelligence agent speaking Spanish, English, and a smattering of other languages. He started learning Spanish as a freshman in high school. He had infiltrated a drug smuggling organization and was involved with making a final delivery to another counter agent from the United States. The other agent had worked with him on other cases with the objective being to not only prevent the drug delivery, but to get the drug thugs arrested. The Agency's plan this time was to destroy the drugs, and get the drug gang arrested by the United States authorities.

This case begin in Peru 6 months after he began with the Agency. He was flown to a small village about 10 miles from the capital of Peru. There, he became an English teacher in a class of Peruvian adults that the Agency suspected were working on a drug farm. They were preparing to become drug pushers in the United States. The English that they needed for this job was only basic. They would sneak across the border from Mexico and make contacts in major U.S. cities close to the border. David's task was to infiltrate the class of students and to report any pertinent drug smuggling information back to the Agency.

David taught for five weeks and was successful in making friends with all of his students. He was also successful in gaining the confidence of the managers of the drug farms. His first break from teaching came when he was asked to travel to Florida to facilitate the transfer of a large shipment of cocaine to the United States. He arrived at a motel and was met by four heads of a drug cartel from four different South American countries.

Somehow, the leaders of this particular cartel received information and had suspected that both David and the other agent were friends. They also suspected that they were drug police for the United States government. Now the leaders planned to do away with both of them. From the interaction with these leaders David sensed this and needed to take some action fast.

The drug deal was scheduled to be completed in a South Florida motel room. It would end up in an unfair battle of 4 against 2 and David knew this.

The six were all assembled in a small motel room with two cases of packaged drugs sitting on the room table. The total value of the drugs was several $millions street value.

The leader suddenly pulled out a knife—a 6 inch edged dagger with a pearl handle. The other three drug hoodlums followed suit and took out similar knives. "Ok," their leader said in a sharp voice. "David and Max are agents from the United Sates and it is judgment day. We are going to cut their throats. You two have double crossed us." Everyone's guns had been checked at the motel desk. A metal detector made sure this was accomplished. The management of the motel had no desire to turn his motel into a haven for gun-carrying hoodlum thugs.

David quickly and silently sent a fast prayer up to his Creator. *Lord, we need your assistance fast. I am ready to meet you, but you may have more work for me and I have some people who need me.* The room was suddenly still for a moment. How exactly the 4 gang members would attack and use their knives was on the minds of the two Agents. David assumed that these men had it all worked out.

"Em nome de Jesus Cristo, congelar!" David yelled out!! There was a slight jerk from everyone. It was as if time stopped for the four gang leaders. They suddenly froze without a movement, their knives held tightly in their hands, and ready to strike. David then calmly walked over to two large cartons of drugs sitting on the table, picked one of them up and started walking to the door. His agent partner followed his lead, picked up the other carton, and walked out the door behind David. They ran to the stairs door and down two flights. They stopped at room 516, opened the unlocked door, and placed the boxes of drugs on the bed. David then went to the phone, dialed a number, and said loud and clear, "room 516. Go!!"

As they drove away from the hotel parking lot, the other agent said to David, "What was that all about, David? What happened? What did you say to the thugs and in what language?"

"The language was Portuguese," David told his friend from the agency. "All four of the hoodlums know that tongue well. What I said was 'in the name of Jesus Christ, freeze!' Right now the 4 gang members are being arrested, and the boxes of drugs are on their way to being incinerated in some fire barrel. Let's get to the airport."

David was soon aboard a commercial flight to Minneapolis. He was very tired and needed rest. It was only a few minutes and he was out. His mind roamed his past from when he was a boy of 4 to the current time. Suddenly the familiar image appeared in the deep crevices of his brain. David had this facial image almost all his life. He thinks he knows where and when the image occurred. Why God had kept it with him, was a mystery to David. It must be for some future purpose, he figured.

*The Garden*

At the airport David contacted the Agency for further instructions. "Hey Max, what's next?" David was Max's number 1 agent, at least the one he liked to assign the difficult assignments.

"You did a good job in that motel room and you succeeded in upsetting much of the drug industries' reorder schedule. But that's good."

"So what's next for me?" David asked.

"I have a difficult one," Max said in a hesitant voice, "one that has been bugging spy agencies worldwide. It involves human trafficking. We have been receiving requests to get involved with trying to make a dent in it or to at least slow it down. None of our agents are trained in this area of evil."

"Where do I start," David asked, expecting to get a specific assignment.

"Well, David," Max replied, "that's my problem. We don't have an exact place for you to start. We have a bunch of heartsick parents who are missing their daughters. You could probably go visit and interview them." David paused for a few seconds and then said.

"Tell me Max, where has the trafficking been occurring the greatest? Let me start at that location and go from there."

"Good idea David. The place to start is here in the Minneapolis/St. Paul area," Max answered. "There have been many stories of missing girls reported. Also, in some cases, parents who have not heard from their girls who have gone to Europe for a vacation looking for a good time."

"Let me start by going to Minneapolis and doing some digging. I will get back to you Max."

David began his investigation of the evil practice of human trafficking by visiting the bus depot in Minneapolis. His thought

*The Garden*

was that the hustlers would zero in on young ladies traveling alone to anywhere, befriend them, make a date with them, kidnap them, and ship them to an auctioneer of sex slaves. There had to be something about a bus depot that made human trafficking easy.

He next visited Max in his Minneapolis office. "Max," David said, "I observed one particular young man who introduced himself to a young well-dressed girl. They talked for a while, exchanged names and said good bye. I can imagine where it could go from there. Maybe they will meet in another city. Who knows? What did he promise her? These kids are looking for a means of escape. These ruthless people with phony but pleasing personalities say they can provide the young girls and boys with answers to their need to escape. Exactly what they need to escape from could be a multitude of reasons."

"Keep digging David, you're on the right track." Max concluded.

David next went to the airport and with the help of airport officials gained access to a boarding gate area going to Europe. There he observed a couple of suspicious characters who mingled with various people traveling to the same location. *A perfect setup*, David thought.

Suddenly, he spotted a man sitting and reading a magazine. He continued to observe the man's face and couldn't help but feel he had seen it before. Then it happened. He forced his mind to recall the recurring image of his youth. In the process, David compared the face of this man with his recurring image. Could this man be the face of the recurring image having gotten much older, many years later? Maybe it was the same man that killed his mother. He stood up and moved a few seats closer to him. The man soon put down his magazine and brought up his cellphone. David listened as closely as the noise of the airport gate crowd permitted. The words that David heard above the noise of the crowd were: "3 girls, Friday, about 18 years of age, and a good price." David suddenly realized why the recurring image was kept in his mind all these years. With his cellphone, he took a video of the man boarding the plane.

That evening he spent time putting his thought together and e-mailed a report to Max.

David's call to the Agency resulted in him traveling next to Alaska. A group of drug trafficking individuals were about to ship a huge amount of various illegal substances into the lower 48 states from the orient. He was one of several Agency personnel who were assigned the task of stopping this shipment.

The Agency knew where the shipment was and when the movement of the drugs was scheduled to depart Alaska. The mode of how they would be shipped was yet to be determined. The Agency force met in a motel to plan the strategy for making the project a success. David suggested to the group of 5 agents that the best plan would be to surprise the drug gang where they were located. Their hideout was in the town of Sven, Alaska.

The leader of the Agency force stood up and spoke. "We will all dress in hiking apparel and ride the ferry to the town of Sven. From there, we will hike to their hideout—a small cabin, about two miles into the woods. We will then use a couple of explosions to scare them out of their cabin, while at the same time set the cabin on fire. Then, as they exit the cabin shooting their guns, we will shoot them in their legs. We need to take these gang members alive. Interrogating them will glean us a goldmine of information."

The Agency strike force was soon on their way and approached the small cabin in amongst the thick forest. It was dark outside and not too easy to approach the cabin to plant the explosive charges. The force had night vision goggles to aid them. It was unknown just exactly how many men and/or women were in the gang inside the cabin. The strike force made the decision to not give them any chance to surrender, since a recent fire fight between this gang and a comparable gang from Brazil had left

*The Garden*

all of the Brazilians dead. The leader had hatched this plan of attack just hours before in a motel room so no one could have knowledge of it. The Agency had discovered that some of the Alaskan drug officials were monetarily involved with the sale and movement of drugs.

At 7 am, the first explosive charge was detonated. Soon one by one the gang came running out of the cabin with some of them drunk, and all only partially dressed. There were 6 of them. The explosion had started the cabin on fire so they were discouraged from reentering the small building. They had their guns and were shooting. The fire provided some extra light needed to see. The strike force took careful aim and opened fire on the legs and feet of the gang. They were all soon down on the ground—most of them unable to move.

David called for a helicopter and Alaskan drug authorities to arrest the gang, along with a medical team to treat their wounds. Once the gang members had been airlifted out of the area, David and the Agency strike force moved in to make certain the drugs inside the cabin were indeed burned.

David had not been home for a year. He had gone to work for the Agency right out of college. Several times he wanted to go home but his work would not allow him. His father understood David's situation and some of the details of his work. It was extremely secret. David flew into Minneapolis on a military aircraft. He then rented a car.

The first place he drove was to a drug rehabilitation center in St. Paul to see his childhood friend, Angie. She had been sentenced to a 5-year term for using and attempting to sell drugs in their hometown of Dalestown, Minnesota. David kept in touch with what was happening on his home front thru his father using a secure satellite phone connection. The agency allowed him to do this as one of his benefits.

His G.P.S. directed him to the building that housed the center where Angie was staying and receiving treatment. Angie had no idea where David was at this time, what his work was, and for whom. All she knew was that he had joined the military when he had completed college and his work was secret and sometimes dangerous. She really did not care to be concerned about him. Her childhood memories were not pleasant and she somehow blamed some of them on David and her own mother.

He parked his car in the parking lot and walked into the building through a set of secured double doors. A guard and a receptionist were the only people in the entry room. David worried that he may not be permitted to go any further to see Angie, but he had to at least try.

"Can I help you?" the woman receptionist asked.

"Yes," David answered. "I wish to visit with Angie Smith." David was dressed in his military uniform that he used occasionally to hide his occupational identity, hoping that the receptionist would be impressed.

"What is your name?" she asked.

"My name is David Norby. Angie Smith was my childhood friend and back alley neighbor. We both graduated from high school together, I started college, and she moved to the twin cities. I joined the Army after completing college and then took a job. I have had no contact with her for 4 years. Then I found out that she is here, and I wish to see her." He stopped at that point and waited for the woman's response.

"Let me get her counselor," she responded. "Just have a seat." Various people walked into the facility while he waited, which David assumed were counselors or instructors. Each one had a card that they showed the receptionist. She then pressed a button which released the door they passed through. Soon a woman came through the same door and approached David.

"Hello," she spoke, "my name is Gloria Hunter and you wished to see Angie Smith?"

"Yes, ma'am," David answered. "She and I grew up together. I haven't seen her for 4 years and wish to talk to her. I also have something I want to give her."

"Well, we are very strict about visitors from the outside for some patients," the woman said. "What I can do is to let you visit her with one of our counselors present in the same room."

"That would be fine, Ma'am," David responded.

"Also, we will have to check out what you want to give Angie," the woman replied.

"That will be fine also," David answered as he gave the woman the bag he was carrying.

"Follow me and I will bring you to the visitation room," the middle aged woman said. David followed her through the secured doors, down a long hall, and into a small room. "I will be back with Angie in about 5 minutes. I think that she is in a class at this time."

David looked around. The room was quiet—probably sound proofed, with cameras and hidden microphones. One single artwork was hanging on the wall. It was of a mother bear and her two cubs. This scene was familiar to David. He remembered the time when he and Angie had been walking in the woods in northern Minnesota, when they came upon this very scene. Angie became frantic and David grabbed her, hugged her, and quickly placed his hand over her mouth. The mother bear and her cubs soon walked out of the area.

Soon the door of the room opened and in walked a different woman followed by Angie. She sat down at the table across from where David was sitting. The woman sat down at one end of the table. As she passed David, she handed him the bag that contained the items he wished Angie to have. No doubt they had been carefully examined. "Angie," David said as he reached across the table, stood up, took her right hand, and kissed it, "it is great to see you. I have missed you." He then sat down.

"Why are you here David? I don't care to see anyone from my past, including you. I don't even want to see my own mother." David was quite surprised at what she had just uttered and wasn't sure how to respond. He just closed his eyes and sat for a few seconds. Then he smiled.

"My dad told me you were here and I am on my way to Dalestown, so I wanted to stop and see my best childhood friend. I have good memories of you. I also pray for you every day"

"I wondered how long it would be before you brought up religion," Angie commented. David didn't know how to respond to that comment either. *Angie had not changed since high school,* he thought.

Why are you so unhappy, Angie?" David asked. "This is not the same Angie from my childhood, or maybe it is. What can I do or say to cheer you up?" He sensed that Angie was putting on a front of her feelings for the benefit of her councilor.

"For one thing, don't you dare mention God's name," Angie snapped back. "You did this many times when we were in school. I blame God for allowing me to be in this place." There was another very noticeable pause in the tense conversation. David thought back to their childhood. In a way, he couldn't blame Angie for what she had just stated. Her only exposure to God came from their church and David himself and it had not always been positive. She probably viewed David and some of his childhood church friends as preachy and religious fanatics. He suddenly realized that nothing he could say would cheer up Angie.

"So what do you want to give me?" Angie asked in an abrupt change in the conversation. She seemed to relax and began to become more accommodating.

"It's something that I believe you could use," David said gently. "You may not appreciate it, but think of it as a present to you from your best childhood friend." He handed the bag to Angie while the woman counselor looked on with interest. Angie slowly opened the bag and took out a large bag of assorted jelly bean, took out a few, and popped them in her mouth. No doubt the woman counselor had also popped a few in her mouth to see if they may have been laced with a drug.

"You remembered that I like jelly beans," she finally voiced something without a frown on her face. She looked into the bag again and pulled out a red box. She opened the box. It was a study bible. Angie rolled her eyes. "I should have known. I probably will not read it but thanks anyway for it, and for the jelly beans."

"I would like to write to you if you will let me," David suggested.

"You may if you wish," Angie answered, "but don't expect much in return. This place is not conducive to writing letters. I really didn't have a very happy childhood. If it wasn't for you my younger years would have been a total disaster. You helped me with my studies and encouraged me to keep on keeping on. I was sometimes mean to you and for that I am truly sorry. Can you ever forgive me, David?" Angie had suddenly shown a positive side to her personality with a happy verbal response.

"Angie, I have forgiven you long ago." She just looked at David and sat quietly for a full 15 seconds. In her mind she was wondering how he could forgive her even before she requested it. "I need to ask you to forgive me also. I was not the nicest boy in our class, which you no doubt remember."

There was one other thing David wanted to do prior to his leaving Angie. "May I pray for you before I leave?" David asked. He left only a few seconds for her to respond. He was almost sure that her response would be negative once she thought about it. David quickly reached across the table and took both of Angie's hands which just happened to be outstretched toward him. As he held both her hands tightly she tried to pull them away. He could feel the tenseness emanating from her entire body through those hands. *There is a war going on inside of Angie,* David thought to himself, and he knew what it was.

"David," she said as her voice quivered. He never waited for her to complete whatever she wanted to say.

*"Lord, Angie is one of your children and we were best of friends as children growing up. I am so happy that I was able to see her at this time. Bless her as she works and studies in this facility. Bless her teachers and counselors and give her and them wisdom and understanding. Help her to read the bible I gave her. May she at least read the notes I placed in various places inside of it. Bless also Angie's mother, my dad, their marriage and their garden. Protect them and provide them with the finances needed to keep*

*them happy. One more thing, Lord—motivate Angie to pray for me as I travel in my work in dangerous places. Amen."* David squeezed Angie's hands once more. She had quit trying to pull away from him and suddenly squeezed David's hands in return.

"Good bye Angie," David said to her.

"Good bye, David," Angie said in return. "Thanks for coming." Angie got up from her chair, looked at David, and walked toward the door she came in through. She turned toward him once more and asked, "What did you mean by dangerous places, David?"

"Sorry, I cannot say. May God and your prayerful thoughts protect both you and me."

David walked to his car knowing that his love for Angie was stronger than ever. He needed to inform the agency of his visit to this drug facility, although they were probably already aware of it.

The agency that he worked for allowed David to have two weeks off twice a year. It was up to him to decide when he took those days off. The only stipulation was that the Agency had the right to interrupt his time off with an emergency case. On his first week of this break, he decided to spend time as the spring planting season was in progress, and the second week when the garden harvesting time was being done in the fall. He would travel to his home and help Helen and his dad with the garden. This plan would not always be possible, depending upon where he was in the world and what his assignment would be at the time. Even at this time he could get a call from the Agency with an emergency assignment.

His mind went back to the scary episode in the motel room. Even when God's protection was experienced he could not be released from the fear of having something really bad happen to him. He thought of the other Agents telling him about the torture that occurred to agents by their abductors attempting to obtain information from them. *Maybe I should just not be fearful and let God protect me whenever a horrible situation occurs,* he thought to himself. But that kind of mindset would not cause him to call out to the Lord each time. *Maybe God enjoys protecting me and rescuing my hide,* he thought.

He thought about the recent time when he and another agent were threatened by some wild crocodiles. They had just managed to escape out of the water's edge in the flooded city of Gambela, Ethiopia while trying to prevent a trio of drug smugglers from shipping packages of drugs to the United States. David escaped without any injury. His partner had his entire foot bitten off. Luckily a medical missionary was visiting the same town and gave first aid to the other agent. The missing foot was never recovered.

He drove toward his home in Dalestown, Minnesota. He wondered how the town had changed since he was last there. He wondered if the garden was still there. David was interested in getting his hands once again in soil and working in the garden. He had only one or two weeks to spend and then it was back to work in some other assignment. After his close call in Florida, David wasn't very excited about thinking what other peril he may next face.

On his way while driving through central Minnesota, he suddenly heard one of his rental car tires blow. He drove to the side of the road, got out of his car, walked around the car until he found the flat tire. He stood looking at the flat wondering if he should indeed struggle with changing to the small doughnut spare, call for the AAA service, or have the Agency send out a repair crew. Then he thought—*it would be costly to have a service or the Agency come and fix the tire when I can do it myself, especially out in the middle of the country.*

He looked around to see where he was. First, he needed to drive the car off of the main highway. He drove the car to the next road, turned on to it and stopped by a mailbox. Pushing the

*The Garden*

---

trunk release button was easy. As he exited the car, he was met by a woman and a teenage boy, whom he assumed was her son.

"Can we give you some help sir?" she asked in a helpful voice.

"You are probably pretty busy people, so I will attempt to change the tire myself." David didn't wish to bother the mother and boy.

"Actually, we were going over to our new garden to do some planting. My son and I want to do some gardening and hopefully be able to sell some of the produce to make some spending money and maybe win some ribbons at the county fair." David had a thought.

"Tell you what," he said to the young boy, "you help me change my flat tire and I will help you and your mom plant the garden."

"Deal," the boy said as he held out his hand.

"Deal," David responded, as he slapped the boy's hand. The mother wasn't too sure of the trade, but she decided to take a chance. They spent the next 10 minutes changing the tire, including placing everything back into the trunk.

"Now, what are we going to plant in your garden?" David asked.

"We want to plant vegetables that will sell on a stand that Jerry will build," the mother said in a happy tone of voice. David took the boy's hand.

"Hi Jerry, my name is David. Do you have a good selection of seeds?" he asked.

"We do sir," the mother responded, "carrots, tomatoes, watermelon, cantaloupe, potatoes, and sweet corn. The tomatoes and cantaloupe are plants. The rest are seeds."

"Great!" David responded with approval. "Lead on and I will do whatever you tell me to do."

"But sir, you have a job or family you were going to see when you had your flat tire. You need to be on your way." It sounded as if the woman didn't want David to waste his time by helping them. *She is probably being protective of her boy*, he thought.

## The Garden

"Don't worry. I am on my vacation and helping you folks garden would be an added bonus to my time off. I just have to make a few phone calls at some point."

"But the planting will take us several hours," she voiced opposition once again, "we will need to work on planting tomorrow also."

"Not to worry," David replied, "I will sleep overnight on your beautiful green lawn or in my car. All I will need will be a good Breakfast. I will even help your husband with the farm chores." There was a brief silence and look of sadness on the faces of both the mother and son. David wondered why and suspected a sad story.

"I do not have a dad anymore," the young boy said. "We buried him over in the church yard last summer." David looked at the mother.

"I am truly sorry, ma'am, I had no idea."

"That is alright, how could you have known?" the mother responded. "He died of a brain tumor, but he was ready to go."

"We will see him again someday," Jerry added.

"David, we want you to stay for supper and you may sleep on the bed in our porch. That is if you are not bothered by the traffic going by on the highway and the coyotes howling close by."

"No problem ma'am. I've been in foreign countries and slept in tents on the ground with hyenas howling"

"My name is Henrietta, David," she responded. Henrietta was an attractive woman in her early 30s. She had dark hair and was well proportioned, having kept her weight from getting away from her—probably from farm exercise and healthy eating.

"Let's get started, where's the garden?"

"This way," Henrietta responded as she pointed north and began to walk. The three country gardeners walked for a short distance into an open field. There, with well divided areas of well plowed soil and separated by short 24 inch high fences to keep the rabbits out, were the plots ready to be planted.

"What should we plant first?" David asked.

"I vote for the tomatoes," Henrietta said excitedly. "David, what is the best way to plant tomatoes?" By her question David wondered if this mother and her son had ever planted a garden before. "This is the first time we have had a garden. We saw this plot in a magazine and laid it out 2 days ago. Then we bought plants and seeds."

"Well, I think the Lord has sent me to you—I know just what to do." For all that day, from noon until evening and from sunup until noon the next day, they planted the complete garden. David also left notes with some key tips on how to take care of the garden. Just after noon lunch, David took them back to the garden for one last thing prior to his leaving. "Now, we need to ask the Lord's blessing on your garden. He got down on his knees and placed his opened palms on the soil. Mother and son followed suit.

"Lord, we ask you to bless this garden, give it rain, your sunshine, and the love from Henrietta and Jerry. Increase the bounty so they will sell much produce at their veggie stand this fall. Also, Lord, protect them from harm and danger.—Amen."

"You know David," Henrietta whispered in his ear, "if I were 10 years younger, I would latch on to you and keep you here."

David bid farewell to his new friends and continued his travel to Northern Minnesota to continue his time off from the Agency. He was hoping that his dad and Angie's mother were anticipating his visit as much as he was seeing them for the first time in a year.

# Chapter 2

**12 years earlier
The Promise of Romance Begins**

It was a beautiful spring day—just after 1 pm. The sun was shining, not a cloud in the sky, a warm southern breeze was blowing, the birds were singing while hunting for food, and the wild flowers were blooming in northern Minnesota. It was the first day of June and the small garden was growing well. Helen and David, the 14 year-old neighbor boy, were busy pulling weeds and watering the garden. "I am so glad that you are willing to help me with the garden, David," Helen said, "Angie does not want to help me. I guess she just hates gardening. I could make her help me but it would not be any fun for either of us and it would be counterproductive. Having someone like you to help me who wants to pull weeds and water the plants makes it so much more relaxing. I start work at the motel at 4 am and get off at noon. By the time I get home I am ready to hit the bed. I just don't feel like struggling with Angie to help me in the garden. You are a life saver, David."

"I enjoy helping you." David said, "Maybe Angie will change her mind someday and start to garden. She is only in the 8th grade, like I am and she is interested in girl things. She'll develop other interests as time goes on, and maybe the garden will be

*The Garden*

one of them. You don't want Angie to help you garden—you want Angie to <u>want</u> to help you garden. Maybe she will change by next fall when we both go into the 9$^{th}$ grade."

"Exactly! What do you want to be someday, David?" Helen asked. She looked on him as a son she wished she had. After pondering the question for a few seconds, David stopped watering the carrots, thought a bit, and answered.

"I think I may try the military or maybe be a teacher."

"I believe that you will do well in whatever you chose to do, David." Helen commented. "I wish my daughter had some of your smarts and good-naturedness. I don't know what I'm going to do with her. I think she really needs a dad."

David had the same thought—*two households could be combined into one.*

Just then, Angie walked out of the Smith's back door and headed toward the garden. David wanted to ask Angie a question. It was time for Mrs. Smith to take her afternoon nap and rest up from 8 hours of housekeeping work at the motel. Both mother and daughter met at the wooden fence gate on the property line. Helen was aware of the fact that David had a thing for Angie. *It is time for the two to talk to each other, whether it is friendly or not,* she thought.

"Mom," Angie said to her mother, "I need some money for lunch with my friends this afternoon. Do you have three dollars?"

"I will get it for you," her mother answered. "Why don't you stay here and talk to David. He is helping me with the garden again today." Angie's mother walked to her house and disappeared through the back door while the two teenagers watched.

"Angie, may I ask you a question?" David knew what her answer would be, but he decided to ask it anyway.

"What now," she answered in an almost angry tone.

"Will you go with me to the carnival on Saturday afternoon? I have some free tickets for 6 rides each." Angie looked at her back door to see if her mom was coming out of the house. She was appearing to be disinterested in David's request.

"No way David!" Then she quickly turned and started walking toward her back door.

*The Garden*

    The Smiths and the Norbys had moved into their respective houses in the late 1980s, the Norbys on Elm Street and the Smiths on Walnut Street. The houses were positioned such that their back doors were directly across from each other. David and Angie were in the first grade when they moved into their new residences a week before they started school together in September of 1980.

    They lived in northern Minnesota on the edge of the small town of Dalestown. The town was made up of the descendants of Finnish immigrants. Both children had a single parent. David was a witness to his mother's tragic murder in the state of Missouri when he was only 4 years old. Ralph Norby, David's father, decided to move to a new location to live. He had decided to raise his only son alone until he was over the tragic crime committed against his wife. Maybe someday he would find some woman he could fall in love with and who would accept David as her own son. Ralph figured that a new home may help them to forget this horrible time in his and David's life.

    David was left with a recurring image of the man that raped and killed his mother. This image would only appear when he was deep in sleep. David never told this to his dad.

    Ralph was a salesman for a hardware distributor and traveled short distances five days a week. He had a 60 year old woman come in during the week to clean and be there when David came home from school and during the summer.

    Angie's mother was also single. Her husband had left her soon after Angie was born. Helen had no idea why he left or where he was. She also decided to raise Angie as a single parent. The only steady work that Helen could find in Dalestown was at the only motel in town. She put in over 40 hours a week and was barely making ends meet. The two single parents were good neighbors, but that is as far as the relationship went. David kept hoping it would go further.

*The Garden*

David was troubled emotionally after his mother had been killed by a transient homeless man walking through the town where his family lived at that time. He sometimes had nightmares, became unruly, and he was hard for his father to handle. His father decided to move to a different town to see if that would help. They moved to Dalestown and became neighbors of Helen and Angie. The move did not seem to help until David and his dad went to a bible camp the summer after the move. It was there that the problem of David's behavior was discovered. At an evening service at the camp, a pastor preached a sermon on forgiveness. Even though David was a young boy, he realized that he could not forgive the man who killed his mom. That day he laid all of the bitterness out and asked the Lord to take it from him. There was an immediate and dramatic change in David's life and behavior.

Helen had started a garden in her backyard. It was done in hopes that the produce would help supplement the food supply in the Smith household. David decided early on to help his neighbor in any way he could. However, he had another objective. Early on he was attracted to Angie even though she wanted little or nothing to do with him. Why she was not attracted to David? One of the reasons was that he was short for his age. She was attracted more to the taller boys in their class. Because of his size, the other boys would occasionally pick on David. However, he was quick and very well built, an indication of things to come as he grew, at least that is what both David and his dad were hoping. His father was 6 ft. 2 in tall. Ralph taught David to be aggressive and how to defend himself.

The other reason that Angie refused giving him anytime in her life was that he claimed that he was a Christian. She had her doubts as she watched how he behaved in school. He was always talking, pulling her hair, playing tricks on her, and doing things she did not appreciate. Of course, she knew that doing these things was not an indication of David being evil, but merely that David wanted her attention. She could not stand him.

Angie's mother soon came out with three dollar bills. Helen slowly handed the money to Angie and stopped short from letting it go from her hand. "Angie," she whispered to her, "we need to be careful how we spend our money. We do not have an unlimited amount, you know." David was busy working, but heard every word that was spoken by Helen. Angie took the three dollars, placed it in her small clutch purse, and trotted off to their back door.

David was interested in earning some money at this time. With what and where could he accomplish this? That is what he was trying to figure out. One night as he lie in his bed, he prayed to God to help him find some work. Then he fell asleep. As he was reading the morning paper, he happened to see an article about a family in Wyoming who had a produce stand along the road selling the produce they had grown during the previous summer. David had an idea. *Maybe Helen and I could sell some produce and we could divide the money in a fair manner,* he thought. He decided he would ask Helen.

The next Saturday morning Helen was in her garden. It was her only full day off from work at the motel. David walked out to the garden and began to help her plant the tomato plants that she had been given at a local grocery store. The store had been delivered more than they had ordered and decided to sell them at a reduced price or give them away. When Helen came in and asked for 5 of them, the store owner gave her an entire flat of 30 for the price of 5. But what was she going to do with them? It would be the first time Helen would have planted more than a couple tomato plants. As Helen was about to plant the first tomato plant, David asked her, "What are you going to do with all of those plants?"

"I really do not know," she replied with a puzzled look on her face. "Maybe give them away." David was ready with a different option. It just so happened that in a magazine David had looked at in the school library on planting vegetables in the spring, there were some good hints on planting tomatoes. The young tender plants need protection when first planted—protection from the sun during the day and from the cold at night. What was needed, the article said, was to place over the plant an empty plastic milk jug with the bottom cut out. In a week or so, the milk jug could be removed and the new plants would survive. It was time to approach Helen with the idea of growing and selling the produce and making some money.

"Helen," David said to his backyard neighbor, "what would you think of the idea of you and I gardening together, opening a produce stand at the end of the summer growing period, selling the produce, and dividing the money in some fair manner? It would give me a job in the summer months, provide our tables with some fresh produce to eat, and give us some spending money. Maybe we could even talk Angie into helping us." Helen stopped her planting tomatoes and looked at David for a full 15 seconds.

"How did you happen to come up with this idea, David?" She asked.

"Well, to tell the truth, God put the idea in my head. I prayed one night that He would help me find a way to make some money this summer. Then I read a magazine article about a family in Wyoming that did open a produce stand and it was very successful."

"I think that sounds like a wonderful idea, David," Helen responded, "and it also answers my prayer to obtain some additional income. Let's do it, starting today. I will have my brother Max bring his tiller over and rototiller my garden plot large enough to take care of all the tomato plants and other plants that we can grow and turn them into a cash crop by the end of the summer."

"How about if we have him rototill up some of our land also," David suggested. "Then we can have even more area to plant vegetables. Also, let's erect an 8 ft. high fence on our property line to grow pole beans and cucumbers of different kinds." Helen looked at David with the look of a mother to her son.

"The motel where I work has a small 8 ft. X 15 ft. storage building at one end of the motel that they are about to tear down or give away," Helen added. "I will ask them if we can use it to sell garden produce. The motel is right along the highway—a perfect location. I'll bet if enough of our church people grabbed on to it, we could move it to where we want it."

"Let me make a couple of suggestion on how to plant those tomato plants," David said. "Make sure that you plant them deep, up to where the first leaves are. Cut the leaves off the stem below that point."

"Why would I do that?" Helen questioned.

"Because on a tomato plant the roots grow out from the stem, as well as from the bottom," David told her.

"Where did you read all this stuff, David?" Helen asked.

"I read it in a magazine I was looking at over in the drug store," he replied. "Maybe I should subscribe to that magazine."

"Well," Helen replied, "that's how we shall plant them. I also have some empty milk jugs that I will cut out the bottoms and place them over the plants."

"One other thing I read in that magazine," David added. "This woman who wrote the article, placed a gallon can, with both ends cut out, around the tomato plants and pushed them down into the soil about an inch and a half. Then, when she watered the tomato plants, she just filled the can up with water. The water would then go directly down to the roots. An added benefit is that the cut worms would stay away—they couldn't get inside the can."

"I will see if I can get some empty gallon cans from Lucy's Cafe, and from the school lunch room," Helen said. "Right now I need to go get some sleep, but I will see you tomorrow. We will talk some more about our proposed venture and partnership."

David continued planting the rest of the 5 tomato plants and spent some time drawing a map of the garden and dreaming how they should expand the growing area. He would need to

*The Garden*

---

wait until the rest of the garden was tilled. He decided to make another trip to the drug store and read more in the gardening magazines.

Just then Angie came through the Smith's back door and walked to the garden. David sensed that she wanted something from him, which was unusual. She rarely said anything to him. "David," she said in an obviously phony nice tone of voice, "can you fix our clothesline so I can hang up some wash?"

"I will do that for you," he answered in a similar phony tone. David walked to the clothesline where the rope had pulled the eyebolt loose from the cross pipe. It took him only a few minutes to place the eyebolt back into the pipe, find, and screw the nut on more securely.

"Thank you for helping me. I have a party tomorrow and I need to wash some clothes for it." David knew that it was her birthday and that she didn't want him at the party. *Her comment was designed to hurt me,* he concluded.

"Well, Happy Birthday, Angie," David said. "I hope you have a good day and get lots of nice presents." He immediately recalled the previous winter when he had his birthday. He had a party and invited many of his friends. He had invited Angie, but she never came. David apparently wasn't invited to her party. *Why would she even tell me she is having a party if she wasn't going to invite me? Maybe she did that to show her disdain for me. Maybe I should get her a present to get back at her—but maybe not.* David had many thoughts, as Angie walked back into her house, most of them not too nice.

The next day, David was out in the garden early. He was busy putting up a fence for the cucumbers to grow. It was also Helen's day off from working at the motel. At about 7 a.m. she appeared out the back door and walked to see what David was doing. "Why the fence, David," she asked? David sensed a slight skepticism in Helen's voice. He needed to explain to her what he was doing.

"If the cucumber vines grow vertical," David explained, "then we will have more garden space. Also, the vines will get more sun and it will be easier to water." Helen thought for a few seconds, then commented.

"That makes good sense, David. You are very smart."

"Helen, may I ask you a question?" he said with some hesitation. "Would it be OK if I gave Angie a birthday present?"

"You surely may do that. Just bring it with you when you come to the party this afternoon." Apparently, Helen thought that Angie had invited David to her party. David didn't say anything to Helen. He had a few dollars set aside for a gift for Angie. He had bought the gift the previous afternoon. David was still in the garden when many of his classmates begin showing up at the party at the Smith home. Some of them saw David, waved at him and wondered if he would soon join them at Angie's birthday celebration. He felt bad and soon walked inside his house and took a short nap. He went to sleep feeling sorry for himself. He dreamed that he was in a foreign country surrounded by wild animals with nowhere to run. He finally woke up when he heard a door shut. It was his father returning home from his sales route. "Why aren't you at Angie's birthday party," he questioned David.

"Guess?" he responded to his father.

"She didn't invite you." Ralph answered.

"Bingo!" David answered. Nothing more was said. Ralph knew the situation with the relationship between his son and Angie. There was none.

The end of that summer.

The body growth of David that both he and his Dad had predicted happened in only 3 months. By the time school began in September David had grown 6 inches and had gained 50 pounds. He went out for football at Dalestown high school and became the star of the varsity team. This was unusual for a freshman.

He was fast and strong. No longer did some boys pick on him. If they did, the consequences were not good for the offenders.

The girls in his class started noticing his pleasing physique, with Angie being among them. She still was not interested in associating with him. He was also the top scholar in his class of 34 students. He was a very busy boy keeping up with the garden, selling of garden produce, sports, studies and church activities. Noticing girls was not high on his priority list, except for observing Angie, any time he had the chance. This was especially true when she was in the back yard sunning herself. David's view of Angie in her bathing suit was instilled in his memory and would keep his mind on her as a romantic item in the future.

Meanwhile, Angie was increasingly following the wrong crowd and slowly getting into trouble. She was also getting behind with her studies. Helen asked David if he would help Angie with her schoolwork. "I will help her, but only if she wants help and if she makes a real effort to improve," he told Helen. Angie agreed that she would make the effort.

Angie causes David an embarrassment.

During January of their junior year Angie stole some money from the class treasury. The money was used to fund parties, dances, field trips, and small appreciation Christmas gifts for their teachers. The money was raised from cookie sales, fall lawn raking, and car washes. The week prior to Christmas the class treasure reported the money box kept in the file cabinet was short a $50 bill. She immediately reported the shortage to their teacher and the teacher reported it to the high school office. They decided to not announce the shortage, keeping it a secret of the principal, the teacher, the treasurer, and one other person. Because of his integrity and character, David was chosen to be the 4$^{th}$ person. They met in secret at the principal's home to discuss the theft. They all promised to keep the theft a secret and

*The Garden*

to keep their eyes and ears open for any information leading to suspects.

About two weeks later David was walking in the back yard when Angie walked out to her back deck. She was taking out the garbage when suddenly David heard some music. It was coming from the coat pocket of Angie. "What's that music, Angie?" David asked loud enough for her to hear him. "Where is it coming from?"

"It's from my new radio I got for Christmas," she answered. That is all she said and walked back inside. David wondered where Angie got the money to buy the radio. He knew she had no job to make money and her mother didn't have the extra money to buy the radio. He wasn't the only class member who wondered about Angie's ability to purchase a radio. Then Angie overheard 3 of the other class members talking about the same issue. Angie became frantic. She decided to talk with the teacher. "Mrs. Cook, I think I know who took the money from the cabinet."

"Who was it?" she asked with interest.

"I saw David Norby using a knife to open the cabinet one night as I walked past the homeroom." Mrs. Cook was quiet for a few seconds and then spoke to Angie.

"Angie, do not tell anyone what you just told me. OK?"

"OK," Angie answered.

The next day Angie told the biggest gossip in their class. "Guess what I just heard? They think that David Norby stole the money from the cabinet at school."

Soon everyone in the school had heard the news, including David. He immediately walked to the principal's office. He knew what to do and talked the principal into bringing in the police to talk. The chief of police was soon in the principal's office. "What are we here for?" the officer asked.

"Take the money box and get all of the fingerprints off of it," David requested. "We will soon find our thief."

"I will need to take it to the Police lab to do that," the chief said.

*The Garden*

"Let's do it," the principal replied. The officer carefully wrapped the money container in a dish towel and headed out the door. He returned in 30 minutes with an envelope.

"I think we have your robber's finger prints. There are two sets, which I am assuming belong to the person who regularly places money in and takes it out of the box. The other set of prints is your robber. Those are just a few prints. "The principal stood up from his desk and called in the 10$^{th}$ grade homeroom advisor, Mr. Nelson.

"Jim," the principal quietly said, "take this ream of paper and this ink pad and get the finger prints from all of the 10$^{th}$ grade students. Have them write their name on the paper prior to placing their print on the paper."

The next day during the first hour class, the principal walked into the classroom instead of the teacher. "OK students of the sophomore class, I wish to announce that the local police think they have determined the identity of the person who stole the money from this cabinet. It is one of you in this room. I will not disclose this person's name, but give him or her the chance to come to me and confess the theft."

The entire class sat quietly as the principal walked out of the room. David knew who the culprit was. He wanted her to confess the theft on her own and repay the money. Everyone in the class knew that a 50 dollar bill had been stolen. Many in the class also suspected Angie as the guilty person.

Later that day David was in the garden harvesting a few of the previous summer carrots under a straw covering, when Angie walked out to see and talk to him. "Hi David," she spoke nervously, "what are you doing?" David stopped what he was doing and looked straight into her eyes. The expression he saw in those blue eyes and on the rest of her face was a guilty look. She looked down at the ground. He knew what she was going to tell him.

"I am harvesting some of last summer's carrots. Your mom and I had a good crop." David said nothing more and waited for Angie to say the next words.

"I need your advice, David," she uttered with her eyes filling with tears. He walked close to her and put his arm around her. "I am the thief and I need to go to the police station. Will you go with me and help me?"

"I will do that for you, Angie," David said to her. "But you will need to repay the money you stole."

"But I don't have any money," she said. "I spent it on the radio. What do I do?"

"Let me go wash my hands and we will walk to the police station and visit with the chief about this matter. I have 50 dollars saved up that we can use to repay the money that you stole."

"I will get some money from my mom to repay you," Angie said to David.

"You need to tell your mom about this as soon as possible," David responded.

After he had washed his hands they headed to the police station. David suddenly grabbed her hand as they walked the 6 blocks to the Dalestown police station. "Angie, let me give you some guidance. I think you need to be as honest as possible, you need to make an apology to our class, and you need to give the $50 back to our treasure in front of the class. This means that you will need to find some small job to make money to repay me."

"Why should I do all of these things?" Angie asked with a hesitant look on her face.

"Because," David responded, "it will help to rebuild your honor and respect among our class and your mom. Keep in mind, the whole town will soon know about your theft and what you do to make restitution will follow you for years in the minds of our class and the town residents. This is a gossipy town."

They soon reached the police station. Angie took David's advice, not only there but also the next morning in front of her class. She stood up and spoke. "I wish to make an announcement," she uttered with a shaky voice. "I am the thief of the $50 bill from the treasury box in the cabinet. I want to apologize to you, my class." At that point she walked over to Clare Wilson, the class treasure and handed over the 50 dollars in ten dollar bills.

*The Garden*

Surprisingly, the class gave her a standing ovation. Her heart and mind for the first time in days became a little more peaceful.

Angie next walked home and told her mom the whole story. They had a good talk and got some conflict issues settled. "Angie," Helen quietly said, "you need to do one other thing. You need to ask God to forgive you."

Angie began to worry as the time for the senior prom approached—she didn't have a date. There were some fellows from other towns that she knew and had dated in past summers. However, none of them communicated with Angie during the year. David wanted to ask her but he knew that she would probably refuse his invitation. Angie was afraid that he would ask her. It was another reason for avoiding him.

It was May 1 and time for May baskets to be made and delivered. This tradition was a big event in Dalestown. Some of the stores carried various supplies to hand make the colorful baskets. David prepared two baskets—one for Helen and one for Angie. He walked across their lots, up to their back door, and knocked.

"Come in David," Helen said upon seeing him through the window. David walked in and held the two baskets up high.

"It's May basket time!" he said. "One for each of you."

"Thank you David. That's so kind of you," Helen said with an appreciative voice. He placed them on the table. Helen took hers and looked inside at the assortment of jelly beans, chocolates, and other edible items. Angie did not say anything and just sat at the table.

"I am also here to ask Angie to accompany me to the senior prom."

"Oh," Angie immediately answered, "I already have a date." Helen looked at her with a surprised look.

*The Garden*

"As of yesterday afternoon, you were without one," her mom commented with a confused look. "Well now you can wear that beautiful dress that I bought for you. I was wondering if that money would be wasted." David continued to just sit at the table without saying a word. After another few minutes he had been embarrassed enough and decided to leave.

"I need to go, so goodbye."

"Goodbye to you too, David. Thanks for the May baskets." Helen voiced gratitude for both mother and daughter.

It was now the day of the prom. Angie still did not have a date for it. David knew this from the grapevine at school but did not say anything. He decided to do something nice for her that was designed to make her make a decision concerning his desire to take her to the prom.

That afternoon she was out in the back yard sunning herself with not much clothing. The weather was very warm and Angie had on a new bathing suit that her mother had bought at a rummage sale across town. David walked out his back door and presented her with a beautiful corsage made of small pink roses and purple violets. "Angie, this is for you to wear tonight. I hope it matches your prom gown."

David guessed what was about to happen. Her situation was now desperate and she was backed into a corner. David was her only escape. "David," she said softly with her voice breaking, "I have no date, will you take me? I promise I will not embarrass you."

"Gladly, Angie. I will pick you up at 6 p.m."

David continued helping Angie with her school work after school and on weekends. She needed to take one class over during the month of July. This help went a long way to insuring that she would graduate. Helen was surprised that she did pass. There were 34 students in the graduating class.

David ended up at the top in his class by the time he graduated, with Angie just barely passing. One week after she had received her diploma she left Dalestown for a job in the Twin Cities area. Angie's mother was very disappointed and was now alone in her house.

David worked hard during the summer in the gardening business and helped Helen make it into the most popular garden stand in the county. Both he and Helen began to worry that as David began his college career, the business would eventually die. In the 4 years of high school, the business had generated several thousand dollars to add to Helen's income and for David's college fund.

It became a matter of prayer for David. He asked God for both wisdom and ideas on how to handle this concern. Just before he began football practice at the college he had picked, he was given the perfect solution.

David and Helen were in a continuous battle with the neighborhood rabbits eating the garden veggies. One day he took his BB gun and shot at two rabbits standing next to each other. He hit and killed both of the furry little creatures. It was the matter of 'killing two birds with one stone.' "That's it," he said out loud.

The work in the garden and the Veggie stand needed someone to replace David. His dad would be the perfect answer. Ralph had weekends in which he only played golf and helped around his church. He was also home most week nights.

David knew that his dad was a lonely person ever since his wife had died. All David had to do was to play cupid and get both Helen and his dad together. Maybe some romantic sparks would fly and they would get married.

David talked to his father about helping out with the garden business. His father, for some reason became interested in the idea—an answer to David's prayer, but maybe because he was essentially done with raising his son. At the same time Ralph suddenly began to notice Helen as he worked in the garden. It wasn't long before the interest became mutual. He began to spend less time on the golf course and more time in the garden. Helen spent time teaching Ralph about the basics of gardening.

Their relationship extended beyond the garden. Soon they were eating together in each other's kitchen. They began to watch television together, attend church, go shopping, and exercising at the local wellness center. Since they were both Christians and went to the same church, they had a destiny ordained by God Himself.

One day about a year after David's first year at college, Ralph took Helen's hand while she was spreading grass clippings between the rows of tomatoes, and slipped a diamond ring on her finger. "Helen," he said in the unromantic setting, "will you marry me?" Helen was not surprised, as the two of them had been talking about it for months.

"Of course I will," Helen responded. "Let's celebrate by having a picnic in the park this noon. We can plan the whole event."

They didn't waste any time and were soon married by the pastor in their church. David and Angie were part of the wedding.

David continued his education for the next two years. He ended up near the top of his college class. His major was engineering and economics. He also took some agriculture classes. He had finished college in 3 years by going to summer school. He continued to make some contact with Angie through Helen and an occasional letter. There was rarely a reply from her in his college years. He did see her once at a Christmas family gathering in Dalestown. She was looking older than what David thought she should look. He attributed this to the lifestyle that Angie was probably involved with. Meanwhile, he kept up his praying for her.

One day he was visited in his apartment by a man dressed in a blue suit with a military tie. It was during his college graduation day. For some reason the man knew all about David. "Mr. Norby," the man said, "what are your plans for the future, now that you are done with college?"

"What is your name sir?" David asked suspiciously.

"Kirby Olson," the man answered. He was about David's height and build. He carried a briefcase and wore sunglasses.

"I have not really decided yet—maybe the military. I may even go on to further education."

"I have an option for you," the man responded. "How about a career that will give you travel, intrigue, good pay, excitement, and opportunity to strengthen our national security?" David looked at the man for a few seconds and then responded.

"Are you suggesting that I become a spy of some sort?" David answered with a sudden look of doubt. "I will bet the job also has some risk."

"Well," the man answered immediately, "let's call it a spy and counter-spy job. It would be in the intelligence gathering field. Tell me David, have you ever heard of the terms industrial espionage, human trafficking, illegal drug trafficking, and other such evil activities?"

"I have and I have read about them."

"Well, if you come to work for us that will be at least a part of your job," the man commented.

"Let me give it some thought." David said. The man handed David some printed material and bid him farewell. It was what David had in mind for his first job. As the man was walking out the door he turned around.

"One other thing. For some unknown reason we have many more women who qualify to be agents than men. We have dug into your background and found that teaming you with a woman partner would be a benefit to both of us. You apparently have high moral principles and could be trusted to be teamed with the girls. That is why we really want you to come and work for us. You would be very trustworthy." He said no more and left.

*The Garden*

After college David took a job with an international firm, which turned out to be a front for the Agency. He was trained for 3 months in Iowa and then traveled to Africa for his first assignment. The training period was most difficult for David and was very hard for him to keep from resigning several times. Many of the new recruits did resign, some of which were female recruits. But he hung on and made it through. He was soon to learn that the 3 months training was for an industrial spy agency with avenues into the illegal drug trade, kidnapping and human trafficking trade, and industrial spying.

Because the work he was training for was so secret, he was unable to talk about it or write about it. He made a few friends but was very careful not to say too much or ask questions. It was a good move on his part since mixed in with the 25 recruits were some who were also undercover plants. Their job was to weed out any recruits that would pose a risk to the Agency.

David was told that he would be airlifted to a place where he would be given his first assignment upon landing. It was the South American country of Peru.

This was his first assignment and he wondered how his Christian beliefs would be tested. Could he withstand the temptations that may present themselves and tasks that tested his Christian and moral character? He would soon find out.

# Chapter 3

David's stop at Angie's rehab center had been what he had expected. She hadn't changed much from high school, but he was glad he had stopped. On the travel to his hometown he couldn't get her off his mind. She was a troubled girl with a war going on inside of her. He wanted to get married someday, but his current work and Angie's spiritual situation made it impossible. *Maybe someday Angie would straighten out to the point where marriage would be possible,* he thought. If she kept going the way she was headed, she would probably end up as damaged goods. God would need to keep her in His hands and protect her, as David had been praying. *Maybe God has someone else for me if and when I decide to settle down,* he thought to himself.

David's father was glad to see him. Helen came out their back door to give him a big hug. "David, guess what day this is?" Ralph announced. "Today is Helen and my 4th year wedding anniversary."

"Congratulations," David replied. "That was in the plan."

"What plan was that?" Helen asked, although she knew David's manipulative spirit.

"What I planned for you two before I went off to college," David answered. "It all worked out."

The Garden that David and Helen had worked on since he was in the 9th grade was growing better than ever and the

*The Garden*

produce stand was producing a better than expected amount of money. It was the middle of June and everything in the garden was growing fast. It had been expanded to cover both backyards. Ralph had moved into Helen's house and he rented his house to a family of 6. He and Helen had pooled their resources and paid off the mortgage on Helen's house.

David spent the next 2 weeks working on the garden and produce stand. He added two more sections of fence to plant a middle of the summer crop of cucumbers and pole beans. He also planted two late crops of bush beans in two raised beds that he built with scrap lumber from a house on the next block that was being gutted and rebuilt. In order to make the raised beds last an extra two years from rotting from the inside, he painted the inside of the 4' X 8' raised beds with a latex paint. The beds were 30 inches high. In order to cut down on the weed growth in the garden, he collected grass clippings from the neighbors and spread between the rows of plants.

The raised beds needed to have at least 5 inches of good soil. The existing soil was mixed with a variety of composts. He collected grass clippings and bags of fall leaves to pack in the beds. When no more grass and leaves could be packed into the beds, he spread the existing soil mixed with compost and various animal manure on the bed.

Some of the early produce was ready to be sold. David and Helen picked every morning while Ralph sold the produce in the produce stand. In addition to selling bush beans, a variety of herbs, green onions, and some ripe tomatoes, they were now selling three kinds of coffee and a variety of cookies that Helen made in her kitchen. The highway traffic was quite heavy on the weekends and people made this veggie stand a regular stop, especially for the coffee and cookies. It had become a popular stop for tourists traveling through the area. At one point after the third day David sat on a chair in the middle of the garden and daydreamed of what he might do some day after his stretch with the Agency. This would be on the short list.

Helen and Ralph took a short vacation during the last week of David's vacation leave from the Agency. As soon as David had arrived home he contacted the rehab center where Angie was receiving treatment. He requested that Angie be permitted to leave for a one week break to her hometown, Dalestown. It was a long shot and he was expecting the answer to be negative. He decided to not tell Helen and Ralph of the request in case it never happened.

Imagine his surprise when he received a reply e-mail stating the answer to be positive. In the e-mail, they explained that because of construction work at the rehab center it would be a convenient time to permit the requested week's leave for Angie. They also had found out that David was very high up on the security clearance list and could be trusted to be responsible for Angie's wellbeing. Ralph and Helen left town on Sunday afternoon just prior to the evening when Angie was set to arrive at the bus depot. David was there to meet her. The same counselor who David met at the rehab center, had ridden with Angie on the same bus from St. Paul to Dalestown. She had David sign a release form holding him responsible for her safety and safekeeping during her week stay.

"Mr. Norby," the counselor said, "I never realized that you were in the service. Angie should be in good hands." The woman never indicated which service she was talking about. She assumed that it was one of the four military services.

"I will take good care of her," David responded. The woman climbed back on the bus and was soon on her way. She apparently was headed further north where she also was going to have a short vacation.

David took Angie's hand and led her to his rental car. He needed to go over some ground rules with her prior to the start of her leave. "Angie," he said in a voice that was non-threatening, "I need to go over some things that the rehab center and I need to have you do while you are here. I hope you do not mind." Angie looked at David and thought about the many times during her childhood when she paid no attention to him or what he had to say.

"You tell me what to do, David," she said in a submissive tone. "Before I left the center I promised to do whatever I was told to do and to behave myself. What exactly do you do in the military? You must have a lot of pull with some high up people." David knew he was unable to reveal any details of his secret work, but needed to give an answer to Angie that would satisfy her curiosity.

"Let's just say that I was able to convince some people that Angie was a good girl and wouldn't be any trouble," David said in a convincing manner. "You will be sleeping in the basement guest bedroom. I will sleep on the upstairs couch. You will be expected to do some work in the house and wash your own clothes. Also, I need to accompany you wherever you go outside the house. OK?"

"OK," Angie responded agreeably, "but why can't we sleep in the same bed," Angie said in a suggestive and joking manner. David turned and just stared at Angie for a few seconds.

"Why do you think, Angie?" David asked, knowing full well that she knew the answer.

"Maybe because we are not married?" She responded. "I'm sorry I made that comment, David."

"One other thing," David continued, "Your mom and my dad gave me a list of chores to do in the gardens. You can help me with these tasks. Maybe you can help me make the cookies to sell at the veggie stand."

Angie seem to be in a non-combative mood and was even more positive as the week went on. This was a change from the past. David hoped that maybe her time at the rehab center had been good for her. Still, there was something he sensed in her attitude and personality that was troubling her. Maybe he could get it out of her—but she would need to volunteer it to him.

The rest of the week went really well for the two of them. David took Angie wherever she wanted to go, even to visit friends that had influenced her to get into trouble in high school. The two of them went on picnics on two different days. The last day was on the Saturday prior to Angie's last day of her leave from the rehab center.

It was a sunny day. Angie had fixed a picnic lunch and placed it in a brown picnic basket. They walked to the park some 6 blocks away. David carried the basket in one hand and held Angie's hand with the other. It was one of the few times they had held hands. Angie held a blanket and pillow with her free hand. When they arrived at the park all of the picnic tables were occupied. They found a big tree and decided to have their picnic on the ground. Angie spread out the blanket, placed the pillow in the middle on one end, and laid down. David took the hint and laid down beside Angie with his head on the same pillow next to her head. They both closed their eyes and were quiet for a few minutes each contemplating where their lives would take them in the near and far future. David had his goals and Angie was unsure of hers. Neither of them spoke for the next 5 minutes. Both were tired. They almost fell asleep with the birds and children making sounds.

"David," Angie said breaking the silence between them, "exactly what work do you do in the military?" David had expected this particular question from Angie all week.

"I do all kinds of things. Go on missions to various countries, meet with people, write reports, and do some instructing."

"Is any of your work dangerous?" Angie inquired with a very serious tone in her voice. David was set for this question, also.

"To be honest, yes. However, please do not ask me anymore questions."

"Then your work is very secret, isn't it David?" David did not answer. Finally, Angie completed this question and answer session. "I thought so. Would it be OK if I worried about you, David? I've seen movies about the work that you do. Some of them do not turn out very nice."

"If I were you, Angie, I wouldn't waste my time worrying about me, you have enough to worry about. However, you may if you wish. Or, better yet, pray for protection for me. In return, I will pray for your wellbeing and protection." They both remained still for another minute. Finally, David broke that silence. "May I kiss you, Angie? It will help me to remember you when I am at my work in various parts of the world."

"Please do so David," she quickly answered." David's request surprised her.

"In return, I will give you some kisses," she said. For both David and Angie the world seemed to stop. Angie could think only of the possibility of this moment lasting, but only on her own terms—not having to change to David's spiritual way of thinking. David hoped that Angie would someday soon give in and change to God's plan for her life.

After they had eaten their picnic lunch, it was David's turn to ask Angie questions. "Angie, what happened to land you into the rehab center?" She was at first quiet, indicating she was not ready or willing to talk about it. Finally, she began to pour out her disgusting tale.

"I have had this hidden hatred within me of my dad for leaving my mother and me after I was born. I decided early in my childhood to never forgive him for what he had done. I have recurring dreams about meeting him in various locations and wanting to harm him—like beating him or pulling his fingernails out. In many of the dreams he is in danger of getting eaten by wild animals and pleads to me for help. But, I will not help him." Angie began to silently cry. David took out his clean hanky and wiped her tears flowing down her cheeks to her ears. Soon the tears subsided.

"Continue your story," David encouraged. She hadn't told how she got into trouble.

"Well, I figured that the only way to get back at my dad was to make trouble myself. By doing that, in some sick way, I thought I could cause him grief. I wasn't even thinking of Helen, my mother. I began to steal, starting smoking, started drinking, and then the drugs. Suddenly, the roof fell in on me. I got caught by the drug police attempting to sell drugs. The selling of the drugs happened when you were away and I was in Minneapolis." David wanted to interject a comment into her story.

"Meanwhile Angie, your mom, my dad, the people of your church, and especially me, were praying for you."

"I know," Angie indicated with a somewhat appreciative tone. "That is the short version of what happened to me. I have reformed somewhat. I no longer want the drugs or the booze."

"That's a good progress report," David commented, "now you can get on with a more productive life."

"However," she continued, "I still have the hidden hatred for my father and I still have my dreams about him. How do I get rid of them?" David knew the answer, but wasn't sure how to present it to Angie.

"I think you know what the answer is to that question," David offered. Angie just stared at David and gave him a gradual hardened look.

"You're going to tell me that Jesus is the answer, aren't you?" she said it in a mocking tone.

"You just answered your own question, didn't you Angie?" David responded. "You see, the hatred in your heart and mind targeted at your father is poisoning your entire life. You need to get rid of that hatred and you are unable to do that on your own." Angie suddenly turned away. She had had enough of that subject, although she knew that David was correct in his analysis. *This session has made more sense than all of the shrink sessions at the rehab center put together*, she thought to herself.

"Time to go back home," David said as he stood up. They walked back to the house, but were not holding hands. There were few words spoken. When they arrived back at the house, Angie went right to her room and climbed into bed. She had a lot to think about.

David contacted the Agency to get caught up on the latest news in the areas of the world where evil was buzzing. "Hey Chief, what's new."

"How was your time off David?" his boss at the Agency asked. "Are you ready for some more excitement?"

"I take it as it comes," he answered with a slight laugh. "Do you have anything that has to do with growing plants in a garden?"

"Maybe?" the boss responded.

"What do you mean maybe?" David questioned.

"Can't tell you now — just wait a while." David became curious.

The car that David rented to travel to his home all of a sudden became disabled when the transmission's reverse quit working. He decided to leave the car in Dalestown to be repaired. The rental car company said that they would take care of its return.

Helen and Ralph were greatly surprised to find David and Angie sitting together and watching television in the living room when they arrived home later that afternoon. "Angie!! How in the world did you get here," Helen asked.

"David arranged for me to have a 1 week leave as long as I behaved myself and did not leave out of his sight."

"I'm hungry," Ralph spoke out with enthusiasm. "Let's go eat at Lucy's Diner."

"That sounds like a winner," Helen responded. Lucy's was not far so they walked.

Their time to and from Lucy's was spent talking and bonding as an integrated family. Everything was up for discussion except for David's work with the Agency and Angie's life style.

The next morning it was time for David to head for his next assignment. It was also time for Angie to head back to the rehab center. Since the rental car was disabled, his father was going to take them both back to the Twin Cities. David hated to leave the garden and his childhood home — it was so relaxing and refreshing. For the past week Angie had prepared at least one salad every day from fresh garden vegetables. In his travels to various countries, the food was not always the healthiest. He had to be very careful what he ate and drank to avoid getting sick.

David's dad let Angie off at the rehab center and drove David to the airport in Minneapolis where a plane had been sent by the Agency to pick him up and take him to an undisclosed location. On the way, David and his dad talked about various subjects. The main topic however, was Angie and her life.

"You really like Angie, even though she is not living the most ideal life. What is her future and how can it fit into your future?" Ralph asked.

"I guess I feel several things about her," David responded. "First of all, I feel sorry for her that she did not have the father that would have guided her through her child and teen years. She actually hates her father, wherever he is. Second, if you could have married Helen when her husband left her, things and events may have turned out better." There was a pause where Ralph was in deep thought.

"I think that may have been a tradeoff," Ralph began his comments to David's 'what if' analysis. "I needed to be your dad and your dad only. That may have been selfish of me, but you were my only concern. I never saw Helen as a potential love object to replace your mother and then be able to guide Angie in her difficult and formative years."

"I appreciate that Dad," David responded in a gracious tone of voice. "I am reaping the sacrifice you made in my work. I am in a similar situation as I view the subject of Angie and me. I see her as a person I would like to marry someday and have our children. In the years since high school, I have had many opportunities to have romantic encounters with various women, some beautiful, and some not so beautiful, but God has always intervened and caused me to resist. He has many times put the thought in my head, *Wait for Angie*. However, in her present spiritual condition, marriage is not possible for us."

"That is interesting, David," Ralph stated. "I will tell Helen that. Maybe she will be encouraged to keep praying for her daughter, and you."

*The Garden*

David was told that he would be airlifted to a place where he would be given his assignments upon landing. It was the African country of Kenya. Upon landing at the Nairobi airport he was picked up by a helicopter and flown to a clearing by a river. There he met a tall skinny man by the name of Spenser. It was probably not his real name. However, David actually had a new name also — James Howe. He now had to get used to it. Getting used to a new name was not difficult since that had been part of his training. Plus the fact that twice in prior assignment he had used a different name.

They got into a car and drove for 8 hours stopping occasionally for food and rest. As they traveled, David was able to see both jungle and desert with several wild animals. He kept wondering what he was to be doing in this remote part of Africa. From his experience thus far, the job could be anything. The car finally stopped at a clearing in the forest where he saw a group of sleeping tents in the middle. His mind begin to think of various jobs he would have within such a camp and with the personnel occupying the tents. Maybe it was a group of scientists who were working on a super-secret electronic spying technique. Or, maybe it was a training ground for new agency recruits, similar to his training when he graduated from college.

As David exited the car he was met by a woman dressed in clothes that made her look like a wild game hunter — fitting the Kenyan tourist attire. "Hi, did you have a good trip?" she asked.

"Not very restful, but interesting," David answered, "too many bumpy roads."

"My name is Angela," she told David, looking at him and studying his face. "I am your agent/partner." He knew that Angela probably was not her real name. He needed to give her his pseudo name right away. Of course, he knew that she knew whatever name he gave her wasn't his real name either.

"It's good to meet you Angela, my name is Jonathon, but you can call me John." Angela smiled at David knowing full well

*The Garden*

that both of them were using names that the agency told them to use during this particular assignment.

The Agency often teamed a male agent with a female agent for various reasons. They would pick female agents who had a high moral character. Most of the time they picked well—sometimes there was a mismatch, which in some instances was on purpose for reasons that only the Agency knew.

"What are we doing here," David asked looking around at the tents and to the outside jungle. "Is this a base camp?"

"We are going to train a group of guerilla fighters from the country of Ethiopia," she said in a whispered tone. "They will then go back into their country where they will attempt to eradicate a group of Moslem guerilla fighters who are trying to take over a portion of their country and cause discord for the government of Ethiopia. Yes, this is sort of a base camp." David was puzzled.

"So what is the difference between the two groups of guerilla fighters?" he asked with the look of confusion.

"That is a good question, John," Angela answered. "The group that we are going to train, although they are Moslem, believes in democracy." David had another question, indicating that he had little knowledge of what this assignment was all about.

"Ok. So if this group is already trained in guerilla fighting, what can we teach them?" David continue to inquire.

"We are going to train them in the latest agency communication technology," Angela responded. The answer seemed to make sense to David.

Angela was a very attractive woman—about 30 years of age. David knew he would have a problem keeping his mind off of this beautiful agent. To make matters worse, the person that was quite often on his mind from back home had the same name, although David rarely had called her that, Angela. *Maybe I need to forget about the Angie from my childhood and concentrate more on my work with this Angie*, he thought to himself.

"Let me show you where you can sleep," Angela said to David in a quiet voice. Then she added in a suggestive voice, "It's next to my tent." He wondered if this was a veiled invitation to him.

He needed to keep his mind away from whatever intentions she may have. "We'll start about 8 in the morning by introducing you to the recruits. Then we'll go over everything we intend to teach the men and women."

"There are women in the class also?" David asked in surprise.

"Of course," Angela answered. "They are among the smartest people in Ethiopia. Well, good night John. Have a good sleep." He opened the flap doorway of the tent and slipped inside. He took off his boots and within 2 minutes, he was asleep. He never had time to pray, he was so tired from travel.

At about 3 am, David heard a low roar outside his tent that woke him out of a deep sleep. It was either a lion or a tiger, David guessed. His gun was in its holster and it was loaded. He had placed it under his pillow. He thought about what the tiger may do. Was it hungry, or lost and just looking for the rest of his tiger friends?

"John," a voice called out to him from the next tent where Angela had also heard the animal.

"I'm here," he answered in as loud a voice as not to scare the animal or wake up the recruits in the other tents. They probably heard the animal also. Angela also had her gun out and ready to use.

"What kind of animal is walking around?" she asked in a somewhat scared voice.

"Some type of a male cat, I think," David responded. "Maybe a tiger. I remember hearing that low roar at a zoo when I was a kid." They both were quiet and just waited for a few minutes. Soon the animal was gone. Both John (David) and Angela continued their night of sleep.

In the morning a breakfast was served to everyone from the rations provided by the agency. Then it was time to go to

*The Garden*

work. A large man who apparently had been flown in during the night stood up and began to speak. He spoke in the Amharic (Ethiopian) language with the English translation made by Angela. "Welcome to Kenya," Angela spoke after the large man spoke in Amharic. "Your training will take about 3 days. It will involve learning to use a newly developed cell phone that cannot be detected by any other electronic device. After 3 days, you will go back into your hometowns and search out any clandestine groups who you believe are part of a terrorist group planning a major assault on your nation of Ethiopia. You will then use your new cell phones to communicate this information back to us." Angela knew her Amharic very well and translated it into English without any pauses.

The group then began to break up into 6 small groups with 6 other agents assisting with the training. David started to wonder what his role in this assignment was. Angela, almost immediately, provided the answer. "John, I suppose you are wondering what your role in this project is?" She said in a whispered tone.

"That would be nice to know," he responded.

"There is only one thing the Agency wants you to do," she said. "That is to stay here for the next 3 days and listen for any of the group who may be part of the faction who are actually the enemy. That means you will be walking amongst the group, listening and watching."

"What will you do with them if and when I find them?" David asked.

"We have a plan to handle that," Angela answered. David was afraid to ask, but he knew.

For the next 3 days David mingled with the training group and attached a tiny device to each of their tents that would record the conversations. He also talked to the groups and ate with them. Interestingly, there was nothing that indicated any spies among the groups. It was a solid group of soldiers.

Then one morning, a helicopter flew in and loaded the training group to take them back to Ethiopia. In less than an hour Angela and David were all alone. He was wondering what his next task would be with the Agency. It involved Angela herself.

"Looks like you and I are alone now, David," she spoke in a sultry tone indicating that she knew his real name.

"You are correct, Angela," he answered in a suspecting tone. David had learned from talking to the Agency in the United States that this particular agent was a sensual person. Sometimes this feature was beneficial to the work of the Agency when it involved various intelligence and counter-intelligence work. The trait indicated the true meaning of the term 'sleeping with the enemy'.

"How about if we take down one of our tents and move in together. That way you can protect me in case Mr. Tiger comes back during the night."

"I don't think that it would be a good idea, Angela," David responded.

"And why not?" she asked. He needed to carefully weigh his response, yet do it in a forceful manner.

"For one reason, we would be tempted to do things that are not part of our work with the Agency—things that are actually forbidden."

"We are all alone, so who is going to know," she retorted.

"God would be with us in the tent and I do not want to kick him out. We may need to rely upon Him to protect us from another Mr. or Mrs. Tiger." Angela became quiet all of a sudden.

"Don't tell me that you are one of those religious nuts," she asked with a disapproving expression. "That's a surprise!" David was quiet for the next few seconds while he was thinking of what to say next.

"Let me ask you a question, Angela." David looked at her for a few seconds, then spoke like a debater in seminary. "What is your definition of a religious nut?"

"It's a bible thumping individual who needs a crutch to lean on in life," she answered in a sarcastic tone of voice. David smiled at her and knew he had the right response.

"Let me comment on your definition with a question," David said. "What is it that you lean on in life?" Angela thought for a moment and finally answered.

"I lean on my own knowledge and understanding. When I get in trouble, I think my way out of trouble." David knew from her answer that she was backing herself into a corner.

"So where do you get this knowledge and understanding?" She had no response and was quiet for a short time.

"Let's go for a walk in the jungle so we can say we have seen the jungles of Kenya." Angela clearly wasn't willing to continue this conversation.

"Let's do it," David responded. They started walking with their guns close by them around their hips in holsters. They walked and talked for the next 2 miles making sure they knew the way back to the campsite. After the 2 miles, they were suddenly confronted by a big black female rhino standing behind a bush.

"What do we do now, David?" Angela asked with a scare in her voice. The big creature suddenly began snorting and smelling the air.

"It is a female and I think she is pregnant," David responded. "Just stand still Angela." David whispered. "Her eyesight is poor and she may go around us."

"Maybe not," Angela whispered back, as the rhino began to walk slowly toward the Agency pair with the target in its mind—maybe a meal.

"In the name of the Creator, stop rhino!" The rhino suddenly stopped and David took Angela's shaking hand and began to quickly walk back to their camp site.

"David," Angela said, "what kind of power do you have?"

"It is not my power. It is the power of our creator—yours, mine, and the rhino's." Angela was quiet as they walked back to the camp and to their tents. They both were hot and tired and decided to take a rest inside their tents.

*The Garden*

A sudden beep woke David up. It was the Agency. "David," the familiar voice said, "are you guys ready to travel."

"Yes we are, what do you have?"

"It's in the next country, South Sudan. They are having more fighting and we have a job for you.

"Who's fighting there now? The Norwegians and Swedes I suppose?" David was joking of course.

"No, it's a hired bunch of thugs who are on their way to murder some of the Nuer and Dinka people. When they kill even a few of these traditionally Christian people, entire villages will be vacated—they will be afraid. Even the villages within a radius of 10 miles will take off. Then the Chinese will move in and set up oil pumping stations. It's oil rich country, you know."

"So how do we come into the picture?" David asked, not knowing how the chief would respond.

"Somehow you will need to disrupt the goons before they get to their target and prior to their attack. There are only about 20 men in the group. So, you and Angela should be able to handle them. Good luck. We'll have a helicopter where you are in about 30 minutes to transport you."

"Angela," David yelled out loud enough to wake her up in the next tent, "arise, we have work to do!" She was up and out of her tent in a matter of 2 minutes.

"Where are we going?" she asked.

"We are going to South Sudan," David answered. "A helicopter will be here to pick us up in less than an hour." Soon both agents were ready to go. They even packed up their tents. They would probably need them, according to the people at the Agency.

When the helicopter arrived, both agents boarded, laid back, and strapped themselves into their seats to have a good sleep. The hot climate in Kenya had tired them out. They were soon in a remote part of South Sudan. When they exited the plane they could hear in the distance the noise of drums. "That noise, Angela," David exclaimed, "is the favorite pastime of the Nuer tribe youth. They communicate to each other in this manner— sometimes all night long."

## The Garden

"So what do they communicate to each other?' Angela asked.

"You know," David responded, "I really do not know? That would be a good question to ask them sometime."

"The Agency informed us that we would be let off within a few miles from where the latest guerrillas are in action."

"When do they attact the Villages?" Angela asked.

"'Actually, both day and night. All they need to do is to scare enough people in the villages so that most or all of the town's citizens take off. They will shoot a few people—men women and children. Sometimes they will walk right into a hut and shoot everyone, the entire family. They are some mean killers."

"So, David, what's our plan to disrupt these no good terrorists?" Angela sounded slightly scared by her voice. David recognized this and spoke without showing any fright.

"We need to get close enough to them to find out about when they might plan to attack," David said, "how they are armed, and what their mode of transportation is." Both agents began to walk slowly towards where the G.P.S. had shown them. They succeeded in getting within ½ mile of the gang of thugs. They found a group of bushes that provided them with good protection. Using binoculars, they could see that there were only about 10 men instead of 20. They were in an open truck with what looked like a 50 gallon barrel of gas. "We need to blow up that barrel of gas. I think the gas is probably for the truck, but it could be used to burn the villages."

"How about if we shoot out the tires on the truck also," Angela added, "when the time for action comes.

"Good idea," David said. As it got close to mid-afternoon, all 10 men decided to move into a small grove of trees and cool off, including the truck driver. The two agents waited a while until they guessed that the small group of mercenaries had maybe fallen asleep.

"Time to go to work, Angela," David said. "First, let's very carefully sneak in and place some explosives on the gas barrel. Then we'll place 6 additional charges on the ammo cases, setting them to go off 3 minutes after the gas blast. They will try to save the ammo cases when the gas blast goes off. I would rather capture the thugs instead of having them killed, but we will do whatever happens."

There happened to be four groups of Sudanese youth communicating with each other with the drums. The noise presented a good cover for the operation. The group of thugs had left their guns propped up against the truck. "Not a smart thing to do," David commented.

Both of them were soon busy creeping very carefully toward the truck to set the explosive charges in place. Once that was done, they moved back to under cover of trees and prepared to start the attack.

The gas barrel explosion rocked the area and the men quickly arose from their afternoon of rest. They all rushed toward the truck which by this time was well ablaze with fire. Angela quickly shot out the front tires of the truck. This was followed by the truck's gas tank exploding. All 10 men were running and attempting to get to their guns by the truck. Three of the men tried to drag the ammo cases off of the truck when 2 other charges exploded. All of the men were soon either engulfed in flames or attempting to run away. The Agency team took aim at the hoodlums running away and fired.

Angela and David did not wait to watch the sight. The rescue helicopter was soon down and they were on their way. As they were flying safely away, David thought to himself—*that is 10 more people I have had a part in killing. May God forgive me.*

"David," Angela said, "I know exactly what you are thinking. You feel that God didn't want you to be any part of the death of these killers. However, this is war and just think of all of the people that may have been killed, tortured, or butchered if we had not stopped them."

They next landed in Gambela, Ethiopia near the Ethiopian Hotel. A room was waiting for them to rest. There were two beds. Once they settled in their room, they ate at the small café next to the hotel. Their meal consisted of a Nile River perch taken from the nearby Baro River. It covered an entire dinner plate. American fried potatoes were on a second plate. Neither of the agents wanted to drink the local water—sickness could result. They settled for a bottle of Amboa, purified water and soda. David had some Snickers bars in his backpack. He gave one to Angela and one to himself. This was their desert.

During the night, Angela suddenly moved over to David's bed and crawled in. He suddenly became uncomfortable. "What on earth are you doing, Angela?"

"What does it look like? We need to celebrate, David."

"Celebrate what?" David countered in a disgusting manner. At that moment, he even thought of pushing Angela out of his bed. But that would not be very Christian, even though he figured under the circumstances God may forgive him. What was really needed was something to happen to convince Angela that what she wanted was something the Agency would look down upon. "What's that noise!!?" David shouted. "Quick let's get our guns." Angela became all tensed up.

"What is it David?" she shrieked in response.

"I think someone is trying to get in here," David answered back. "Let's check it out." David got out of bed, grabbed his gun, and walked toward the door. He opened it and looked out. "False alarm!" Angela suddenly became calm and understood what was taking place.

"OK, David," she said in a meek manner. "I see what's going on. I will get back to my own bed."

# Chapter 4

David survived the temptation to do evil with his Agency partner, Angela, that night in the Ethiopian hotel in Gambela. God demonstrated His power to both of them by keeping him morally pure.

He wondered what he was supposed to do next with the Agency. His answer came as he was reading a portion of scripture on his electronic bible device at 4 in the morning. "Be still before the Lord and wait patiently for him." It was from the book of Psalms. That was his answer.

As he fell asleep, David's thought process brought him back to his secret image of a man. The boyhood image was now added to the airport image of maybe the same man. David had the Agency lab analyze the video he had taken at the Minneapolis airport. He felt certain that he would meet up with this individual someday. He had sent a message to the Agency lab asking them to send any significant piece of information when they found something.

David knew that God caused him to have these images in his mind for a specific future reason. He just needed to wait patiently for the right time.

The two agents ate breakfast in the hotel café, consisting of corn flakes, milk, ham, American fried potatoes, and mint tea. Angela did not say much. She was quite embarrassed from

*The Garden*

the previous night's incident with David. He never mentioned it to her. She spoke little and never even looked toward him all through breakfast.

The sound of another helicopter came into their range of hearing and landed in an open field close to the motel. A well-dressed man emerged from the helicopter while the pilot stayed inside. David walked toward the man and they met by a big tree.

"David Norby," the man said in a deep voice, "I am here to give you your next Agency assignment."

"Thank you for coming," David replied. "I am ready."

"We will take Angela back with us. We will take you into Nairobi to a hotel. There, we will land on the roof and you will walk down to room 325 where you will wait for one day for a visit from a woman who will be your next partner. She and you will work on your next assignment. She will have all of the details."

"Sounds good, Sir."

"Do you have any questions?" the man asked.

"Only one. I have a childhood friend in the U.S. that I would like to communicate with from time to time. Is that at all possible?"

"Is she a relative?"

"She is the daughter of the woman my father married. I grew up with Angie."

"Like a sister?" the man asked.

"Something like that," David responded, "more like a step sister.

"I will see what I can do. We will send you information where you can send a letter or e-mail. What you will need to do however, is to write in the Agency code language. As it is received by your friend, it can be decoded back into English." All three of the Agency agents walked toward the helicopter and boarded. David needed to ask the male agent something without Angela listening. He took out a piece of paper and scribbled a few words on it. *Is Angela trustworthy?* —The note read. David handed the agent the note without her seeing the transfer. Just then Angela got up and headed for the onboard bathroom. The agent leaned over and placed his mouth close to David's ear.

"Did she get fresh with you?"

"How did you guess that," David responded. "I thought that the Agency never allowed people of low moral character to join."

"That's Angela," the man responded. "The agency uses her to gain information from spies in compromising situations. Sometimes she actually kills the spies. She is a naughty woman, and also she has some type of disease. Forget that I told you this. OK?"

"Got it," David responded." He wasn't surprised and quietly thanked to Lord for protection from doing something that could have damaged his reputation and possibly given him something else. Most important, he would have committed a sin.

"I know by your file that you do not engage in such practices," the agent said. "However, the time may come when you may be required to get into a compromising situation to either obtain critical information, kill a spy, or keep from getting killed yourself. At some point a decision will be asked for. I am just giving you fair warning. Do you understand this?"

"Yes I do, sir," David answered, "but God will protect and shield me.

"I understand that your special friend back in Minnesota has been in trouble with the law," he commented.

"To me it's a secret," David responded. "How did you find out that piece of information?"

"The Agency tracks your movements."

"No more discussion. My lips are sealed," David replied." Angela soon returned from the restroom. She leaned down and spoke to David.

"David, you are an honorable person. I will miss you and want to thank you for saving my life at least a couple times. Can you remember to pray for me sometime?"

"Yes. I will do that." David answered. "But you should pray for yourself." She then returned to her seat.

## The Garden

David walked down from the roof of the hotel where the helicopter landed, to room 325. The door was open and a key was on the dresser. He took the key and tried it on the door. It indeed was the door key. He then checked all of the closets and under the bed for any hidden persons or explosives. After locking the room door he laid down on the bed and relaxed for a few minutes. It seemed that the minutes stretched into hours. David was soon asleep.

Two hours later a knock on the door woke him up. He wondered who could be at the door. Maybe it was his new Agency partner a day early. A glance at his watch told him that it was 1 pm Nairobi time. David quickly got up and retrieved his gun. He walked toward the door and called out, "Who is there?"

"Gabe," a quiet voice answered back. "I have some food for you." He had never ordered food. David became a little leery and got his gun ready. He walked slowly toward the door, unlatched the inside chain lock, stepped aside, and aimed his gun toward the door where the man would be.

"Open the door slowly," David said. The door slowly opened and in walked a short dark skinned man pushing a rolling cart with a tray apparently from the hotel kitchen. This was not part of the plan that he was told. If this person was from the kitchen, he would be wearing a white motel uniform. David began to become a little more suspicious. "Can I help you, sir?"

"I was told to bring you this food," the man answered.

"By whom?" David asked.

"By someone who said he knew you," the man answered. Just then David saw at the bottom of the rolling cart a wire sticking out. It was the same kind of wire that was used in plastic bomb construction. David quickly grabbed his leather attaché case off the bed and hustled out the door. In the process he almost knocked the man over. As he began to race down the hall, he yelled back to the man.

"Quickly, get out of the room—don't wait!" He ran to the end of the hall, broke a window, and carefully passed through it making sure he did not cut himself on the broken glass spears. Then he jumped 3 floors down onto the roof a car parked just

*The Garden*

below. As he was half way down, the hotel was rocked by an explosion. He had given the man warning and hoped he had sense enough to escape unharmed. His landing on the car put a big dent in the roof. He jumped down to the sidewalk and hustled down the street.

David walked 6 blocks and entered the American Embassy wearing a baseball cap which was stored in his attaché case. He went to the main secretary's desk and spoke to the middle aged woman sitting behind the desk. "Miss, I need to speak to the highest ranking person in the embassy."

"What is the subject that you want to discuss?" the woman asked. David was expecting that question and was ready with the appropriate answer.

'I need some information on traveling in the country of Kenya. I've never been here before." Those two statements were code for 'I am an agent and need to talk.' The woman quickly walked down the hall to a room and brought back a man that had a slight limp. The man motioned for David to follow him. They walked to a door that led to the basement stairs. When they got to the bottom of the stairs, the man took David's hand and shook it.

"David, it's good to see you once again." the man said. "I'm sorry for the explosion at your hotel. We think we know who is responsible. What we don't know is how they knew you were there. We have a leak somewhere and we will find him or her soon."

"Clyde, I was hoping that I would run into you sometime again." David had not seen his instructor from the Agency training for some time.

Do you have any ideas who the culprits were? The bomb was hidden under the food cart. What happened to the man that came into the room?"

"He died in the explosion. There is no way you could have saved him. The culprits responsible were part of a terrorist group operating about 100 miles from here. That is your next assignment. They are involved in a drug cartel operating somewhere here in Kenya. I have a car for you that will be how you will travel to a ranch. Leave your car 4 miles from this ranch and go on foot. The GPS will guide you. This ranch harvests and packages a drug. The owners sell it to the drug dealers in various parts of the world. Your task is to infiltrate the group using the ranch as a base, and learn as much about them as possible. Somehow, you will need to gain their confidence." David had many questions.

"What kind of terrorists are they?" David asked.

"They are a group from several African countries that are financed by drug producing farms in the region where they are operating."

"What kind of drug?" David further inquired.

"It's a type of weed that is grown only in that region. It has been recently found and has never been classified by plant scientists. They think it has been lying dormant in the ground for centuries. A flood a few years ago apparently jarred the seeds loose from the subsoil. One of your tasks will be to write a report on the plant and present it to the Agency."

"So, what type of behavior does the drug produce on someone who takes it and how do they take it?" David continued his inquiry. His former instructor had the answer ready.

"Some of the people mix it in water and drink it, some smoke it, and some snort it into their nostrils. I suggest you don't try it. You may be asked to try it. Don't do it!"

"So, what happened to the person who I was to meet at the hotel that would be my next partner?"

"Unfortunately, she is now missing. We are looking for her and if we do not find her we will get you another one. Or, she may show up. Supposedly, she has a family in Kenya."

"Let me ask you a question. Why do they pick women to be my Agency partner?"

"I am not really sure but I suspect there are a number of reasons. First of all, the Agency knows that women are more honest and trustworthy than men. Also, many of the cases involve women and a male partner cannot go where the woman may go—like in a woman's room. Finally, in your particular situation, not all men are attracted to women as much as others are. They know that you are a highly moral individual. I have seen it on your file."

David bid farewell to his former Agency instructor and friend. He took off in a rental car down the road toward where a map showed the location where the drug farms were located. As he drove, he wondered how he was going to infiltrate the terrorists. He also wondered why the Agency called them terrorists. Weren't they just farmers growing a crop that could be turned into cash—like tobacco? What is so bad about this drug?

When David was within 2 miles from where the GPS indicated the ranch location, he stopped, turned off the road, drove into a much wooded area. He parked and locked the car, took his bag, and continued walking on the same road. Soon a car stopped and the window rolled down just enough to talk. David noticed that the doors were locked "Sir, are you lost or do you want some wild African animal to attack and eat you? I don't normally stop for strangers, but this area is packed with hyenas" David looked into the car window and saw a very beautiful light brown skinned woman—maybe a mixture of two countries. Her English was very good and her beauty dazzled him for a few seconds. He had a story already to tell her that would give sufficient information to satisfy any questions she had. "What are you doing in the jungle?"

"Actually, I am a plant scientist and doing research on new plants that could be used in making medicine. That is the assignment that my company has given me—Not very exciting, but it pays the bills."

"Hold on a minute, let me drive to the edge of the road." David stepped away as the woman slowly moved the car forward to the edge of the narrow road. "Why don't you get in and we will talk. I think I can trust you." He opened the door, set his bag beside her, got in, and shut the door. She started to drive again.

"Thank you, Miss. I'm a little tired of walking."

"What plants do you expect to find in this part of Africa, walking on a lonely road?" He wondered if he should give her his name and what name he should use. "My name is Madeline," she said as she smiled at David. "My parents have a ranch close by that they inherited from my grandparents. We normally grow grains that we sell to various markets and also raise beef cattle. We are now engaged in raising a new plant that is being seeded, harvested, sold, and exported to other countries. We do not know how they use it—some type of medicine, we think. All we do is dry the plant and box it. Some trucks come to pick up the plant when it is dry, boxed, and ready for shipment. We get paid on the spot, which makes it a cash crop."

The woman was driving very slowly for some reason. Maybe she wanted David to view the countryside, or maybe she was unsure of her ability to drive on such a narrow road.

"My name is Alex Pearson. I am from the state of Montana," David said to his new acquaintance. This was not the truth and he felt guilty every time he changed his name or gave some other false information about the job that the Agency told him to convey. He was a Christian and knew it was a sin to tell a lie. However, his employer told him that in order to protect himself, the other people working for the Agency, and his own family back in Minnesota, he would need to tell a fib occasionally. He felt that God would protect him if he did or did not tell the truth about his identity.

"You are a long ways from home, aren't you," Madeline asked? "What are your plans and where are you going to stay."

"I just arrived in Nairobi yesterday and don't know where to stay. I was hoping I could find a small town with a motel or an inn. If I had a tent I could even sleep in it."

"Fat chance of you finding a motel at this location in Kenya and I wouldn't advise sleeping in a tent," she answered. "Not in the middle of the jungle. There are occasional villages, but not any motels. I do have an option for you, if you are interested."

"What's the option, Miss Madeline?" David responded, suspecting what her response may be.

"You say you are doing research on plants in Kenya?" she inquired.

"That is correct," David answered. Just then Madeline slowed down and turned into a driveway. She reached for a device on the seat and pushed a button. A gate in front of the car began to open. It was then that he noticed that the gate was part of a 12-foot high steel fence that extended for as far as he could see both to the right and to the left.

"If I can trust you, we have a few rooms in our house where our occasional guests stay. You are welcome to bunk with us for a while. You can do your research around our ranch." David thought it strange that she would offer a place to stay to a complete stranger in the middle of Africa.

"My company will pay you the going rate if you could do this," David said.

"We can work those details out later," she answered. The gate closed automatically and the car continued on the long driveway to a big ranch size house. David noticed some buildings off to the side that were painted with a color that approached a barn red. He assumed that they contained equipment for planting, harvesting, and processing the plants. Off to one side was a herd of beef cattle.

"Let me show you where you can bunk while you are here. I'll have our chef make a light lunch for us and we will sit and talk."

"Thank you for your kindness, Madeline," David said.

"Just call me Maddy, Alex," she said.

"Maddy it will be," he responded. She showed him to a room on the second floor that had its own bathroom, a writing desk with a computer, and a Television. *Apparently, they have some type of satellite hookup to get TV reception and Internet connection*, David thought to himself. This would facilitate his work. How he would obtain a secured line to his agency was his next concern. *Maybe they are in an area where the satellite would provide a connection.* After he washed up and changed clothes, he walked back downstairs where he found Maddy sitting on a sofa.

"Is the room satisfactory for your liking?" she asked. He began to wonder what she was up to. Here was a woman

*The Garden*

whom he had never seen before, who picked him up—a perfect stranger—on a remote jungle road, and offered him hospitality that was perfect. It was almost as if it was all planned. Or, maybe it was something the Lord created to test David. *If only she was Angie sitting on the sofa,* he wished. *"But that situation would be off limits for me also,"* he concluded his thought. He had another thought. Could it be that Maddy was an agent in reserve and the Agency had advised her that David was walking on the road?

"Your kindness is beyond what I could ever wish for," David responded. "The room is great. I will need the Internet hookup for my work." Just then an older gentleman in white clothes came thru a swinging door carrying a tray of food and beverage. He set it on a small table in front of the sofa between the two ends where David and Maddy were sitting. The man then walked back through the same swinging doors.

"Help yourself, Alex." Maddy said kindly. "You must be starved. We'll have dinner at about 7 pm." David closed his eyes for about 10 seconds while he asked the Lord's blessing on the food. Maddy noticed David praying.

"Yes, indeed," David responded, "I am hungry."

"I guess you were praying for the food just now, right?" Maddy asked.

"Yes I was," he answered. David saw this as another test he encountered many time before. "I prayed for the both of us."

"Thank you, Alex," she responded. "I told the chef to provide at least 3 drinks for you to choose from," she said.

"Thank you," he responded in a respectful manner, "but I'll just stick with water." Maddy was silent for a few seconds.

"Don't tell me, you don't drink," she said.

"You are so correct, Maddy. I never have."

"Why not," she asked, although she guessed after he had prayed. David needed to be careful how he answered her question. He didn't want to discourage her from continuing her gracious hospitality to him.

"Well," David began while taking a long drink from the glass of water on the tray, "I made a promise to my Sunday school teacher when I was a boy of 8. He was a recovering alcoholic and hadn't taken a drink in years. He said to me one Sunday morning during Sunday school class, "Alex, I will guarantee that you will never become an alcoholic if you promise me something."

"What is that, Mr. Halness?" I answered him.

"Never take the first drink," he advised. "And, you know what? It has worked so far."

"Interesting," Maddy replied, in a manner indicating her non desire to continue this particular discussion. "Tell me about your job and what you plan to do here in Kenya." They had finished eating the small sandwiches. Maddy removed the tray from the sofa, set it on the coffee table in front of the sofa, and moved down to the middle of the sofa.

"Are you married?" David inquired, in a manner which hopefully would tell him if a husband may be entering the ranch house while he is there.

"No, I am not," she answered. "I have been close to it, but withdrew out of the relationship before I made a big mistake. How about you, Alex?"

"Not close." He replied.

"Do you have any special friends?" Maddy asked.

"Maybe," David answered wishing to change the subject as soon as possible. "My work right now is to find new plants around the world that could be used in my company's research for new medicines and other uses. I will be looking at your plants that have been lying dormant for centuries." David needed to answer two separate Maddy questions—the one about his possible love life and the one involving his work. "And yes, I do have a special friend back in Minnesota."

"That's interesting," Maddy responded. "But how could a plant be dormant for centuries? Wouldn't it be growing for millions of years?" David was ready with the answer.

"The answer to that question goes back to the philosophy of my company. We believe in the Biblical creation of the universe and earth. When God sent the flood on the earth, he destroyed the people and animals, except for Noah's family and two of every kind of animal. Only Noah and his family, along with the animals on the ark survived to repopulate the earth. The

*The Garden*

bible does say all of the animals were destroyed, but it doesn't say anything about what plant life the flood may or may not have destroyed. It is possible that the flood he sent buried some plant life in the earth to come forth and be discovered later for reasons that only God knows about. That is where my company comes in." David had suddenly stirred Maddy's interest, as she listened to him intently.

"My Family is involved with such a plant, from what you just described. We discovered it about four years ago as a result of a flood of a creek running about a mile from this ranch. I tasted the leaves and it gave me a feeling that is hard to describe. We waited until the plants grew to the seed stage, harvested them, and saved the seeds. Then we grew about an acre of the stuff and in only 6 weeks we harvested enough seed to sell. It is a very fast growing plant. We have multiple plantings each year."

"Who do you sell it to? "David asked, indicating his desire to probe the possible illegal activity that Maddy's family were maybe aware of and involved with.

"A company in California," she said quietly.

"It sounds like the stuff may have some medicinal uses," David responded, "just what my firm is looking for."

"Maybe we can do business," Maddy replied.

Maddy and David talked for another two hours. "Alex, tell me, do you have a family or girlfriend back in the states?" He immediately sensed where this question was headed.

"As a matter a fact, I have a girl that I grew up with. I went to school with her." He wished to say no more about Angie.

"But you are not going steady with her, right? I can tell by your lack of excitement." David needed to change the subject.

"How about you, Maddy? Do you have anyone on the hook?"

"I have never heard that expression," she answered with a giggle. "Yes, I have had some relationships, but nothing very serious." With that comment David stood up and excused himself. He walked toward his room. He sensed that Maddy was

*The Garden*

following him. As they got to the second floor, Maddy spoke. "If you need anything, just let me know, no matter what time it is." He wondered what she meant by that statement, other than its face value.

"I'm ok," David replied. "Thank you anyway.

As he entered his room he had a buzz on his mobile phone. It was from his Agency boss. "David, I will call you back in 10 minutes on a secured satellite line." As soon as he hung up, he knew what to do. He went to his door and opened it slowly. Maddy was in a room across the hall. He could see that she was working at a computer. He sensed that she might be attempting to intercept his expected call from his headquarters. David's suspicion that Maddy was either a spy or a counter spy was probably about to be confirmed. He suspected it was not by accident that she picked him up along the road.

David woke up the next morning from the noise of a truck outside. He went to the window and looked out. Some men were loading some boxes onto the truck. He needed to find out what those boxes contained. It had to be a product or byproduct of the newly discovered weed or plant. His company would like a sample to do some research. Maddy was the answer to this need. It was 7:30 and Maddy was apparently still asleep. David knocked on her door. He waited for a few seconds. "Who's there?" was the voice coming from inside the room.

"It's Alex." was the reply. The door quickly opened and Maddy appeared wearing only a summer two piece pair of pajamas. "Would you like to go for a walk?" he asked. Maddy stood facing David with a look on her face that indicated that she considered it was too early to be awakened.

"OK, let me quickly get dressed," she answered. David stood in the upstairs hallway and waited. Maddy soon appeared with clothes that were more in line with hiking attire. "Where do you wish to walk?" she asked.

*The Garden*

"I need to see what that new plant is like and what products you are making with it. I hear a truck and see out the window that they are loading some boxes." Maddy still wasn't sure who David was or what he was doing in Kenya. If she was indeed an Agency employee, no one had informed either of them what was going on. Maybe that was what they wanted.

"Ok, I will meet you downstairs and we will go for a walk. I will take you out to see some fields of the plant." Soon she appeared in the living room and was ready to go. David was hoping that they would walk to the building where the truck had been loaded and was now gone. Maddy, however, walked in the opposite direction, out of the ranch gate, and onto a road just wide enough for only one vehicle. "This field here will be harvested next. We need to harvest it by hand since there is no equipment designed to harvest it. At least we have found nothing yet that will do the job." As they walked, David asked her another question.

"This field is outside of the ranch and open to the wild animals. Won't the animals eat the plants?"

"For some reason, the grass eating jungle animals do not like it." Maddy responded. David concluded that maybe the animals were smarter than humans and could not take the buzz that the weed gave them.

"Pardon me for asking Maddy, but what is your ethnic background?" David asked.

"Actually, I am ½ American and ½ Eritrean. My father immigrated to America to flee the civil war between Ethiopia and one of its former states, Eritrea. He recently bought this ranch. I have asked him where he got the money to buy it, but he won't tell me." David drew from her answer, a lie. She had said previously that the parents had given Maddy's dad the ranch.

"I knew that you had some Eritrean in your ethnic makeup," David responded. "Your accent has some of the Tigrinya language in it. So Maddy, what do your customers use the plants for? Is it a food, a medicine, a substance to clean your sink with, or what?" David could see by the look on Maddy's face that she was very hesitant to disclose the real use of the plant. He

*The Garden*

needed to prime the pump. "I heard that the plant is used as a drug by some people." Maddy was suddenly quiet as they were walking along.

"Where did you hear that," she asked with a slight break in her voice.

"My company has information as to this possibility," he answered. "Let me see how you are processing the plant and show me some of the finished product."

"I cannot do that," Maddy replied.

"And why not?" David challenged. Just then an animal noise was heard from the bend in the road just ahead of where they were walking. Maddy quickly grabbed David's arm, stopped him, and tensed up.

"That's the noise that a hyena makes," she cried out with fear in her voice. "There is probably a pack of them."

"What do we do?" he asked with some of the same fear in his voice.

"Let's just stay quiet," she said. "We should have walked inside the surrounding gate. Maybe they will not notice or hear us." They were absolutely still as Maddy's grip on David arm suddenly strengthened into a hug. Her whole body was shaking.

"The pack will smell us, won't they?" he questioned.

"They already have," Maddy reacted. "Here they come." It was too late to run, neither of them had weapons, and there were 6 of the wild animals. David quickly squeezed Maddy and they were embracing each other as a pair of lovers. Maddy was both thrilled and hysterical. David could think of only one thing to do.

*"Lord, quiet the pack of the hyenas and send them away. Settle Maddy's frantic mind. Send us an angel to rescue and protect us."* David and Maddy continued to clasp each other tightly. The hyenas all of a sudden became quiet as they slowed the pace toward their expectant meal. Maddy and David both watched the pack as they all of a sudden stopped. They were only 10 feet from them. Within 15 seconds something caused them to turn around and walk into the jungle where they had come from. David and Maddy released their embrace and began quickly walking back to the ranch.

"Alex, who was that man who scared the pack back into the woods."

"What man are you talking about?" David asked.

"Didn't you see him?" she asked with a puzzled voice and a still scared Look.

"Well no, I did not see anyone, but when I was talking to the Lord, what did I ask him?"

"You asked Him to send down an angel," she answered.

"Maddy, you have just witnessed an angel," he responded. "You saw the angel, I did not." Maddy did not say anything as they walked back to the ranch. They entered the living room and were met by the cook carrying a tray of food which he set on the dining room table.

"Your brunch is served," he told them and then departed into the kitchen. David and Maddy sat down at the table and ate the midmorning meal.

After their brunch, the two of them continued their trip around the ranch and the fields of growing plants. This time they took guns with them and the fields were inside the 12 foot high fence. They spent the entire afternoon touring the fields while talking about various subjects. Both of them dug into each other's educational background without disclosing their exact current careers. The fact that neither of them did this indicated that both were probably aware of each other's spy career connection. When they returned to the ranch house, the evening meal was served by the chef. They were very hungry.

Maddy met David as he was coming out of the living room. They were both headed to their separate sleeping quarters on the second floor. She walked to the door of her room and stopped. She opened the door. He could see the inside of her room. "Alex, will you sleep with me tonight? I am really scared after this morning." David could see that she had fear written all over her face. Her look was genuine, she was not acting. Her voice was honest and he sensed that she had no romantic intentions in her request.

"OK, Maddy, I see that you have a couch in your room. I can sleep on it."

"Oh thank you Alex," she responded in a sudden relaxed voice. Tomorrow we will use an all-terrain vehicle and bring the guns."

"I have a question for you, Maddy. Where are your parents?" Maddy was quick with her answer.

"They are in South America on a business trip. They are supposed to return late some afternoon. I may need to go get them." David read into this explanation that they were mixed up in some type of drug business. David wondered if Maddy knew about her parents' drug connection or if they knew that she was an intelligence agent.

Both hikers were tired and they soon were asleep. David woke up about two hours later from the distant noise a pack of hyenas were making. *It's probably the same pack that we were almost attacked by yesterday,* he thought to himself. David began to wonder why God never permitted him to see the angel that Maddy said she had seen. He had never had that experience. At least he thought he had never seen one.

Early morning began with a loud and sudden crash of thunder. It scared both Madddy and David. She woke up and scooted over to the couch where David was sleeping. "I'm scared of thunder and lightning also," Maddy said. "Add this to my scare list along with the hyenas." David sat up on the couch and put his arm around her to comfort her.

"What time is it?" David asked.

## The Garden

"It is 5 am," Maddy answered. "I'll walk down and see if we can have the chef prepare an early breakfast. I'll get dressed and let's meet on the patio. We can eat while we listen to the rain."

"Sounds good," David responded. "We can also plan what we are going to do today." David hurried and got dressed so he could get to the patio ahead of Maddy. He needed to contact his Agency boss. During the night, he had concluded that Maddy was not telling him the whole truth about her parent's farming operation.

David was able to get a secured satellite connection almost immediately. David reported what he had found out and received some crucial information about his current task—the drug made from the newly discovered plant in Kenya. He closed the call just before Maddy entered the patio.

"It's cool, but comfortable this morning, Alex," Maddy commented. "Did you have a good sleep, at least until the lightning and thunder woke us up.?"

"Yes, I did," David answered. He wasn't exactly telling the truth, but he did get a little sleep. Kenya is close to the equator and when the sun goes down, the light quickly goes down also. The opposite is true in the morning. When the sun comes up, the light quickly appears. They both had gone to bed early.

"Breakfast is served," came the voice of the chef as the door to the patio opened.

"Good," Maddy responded, "I am starved." On the tray was a typical American breakfast—scrambled eggs, toast, crisp bacon, orange juice and coffee. The chef departed through the same patio door. David folded his hands and was about to pray. "David, go ahead and bless the food for both of us."

"Surely," David answered happily. *"Lord, bless this food for both Maddy and I. Thank you for sending an angel to protect us yesterday. Protect us again today. Thank you for making Maddy a good friend to me. Bless my family and loved ones back home. Amen."*

"Amen," Maddy added.

*The Garden*

"What family do you have back home, and does that include your girlfriend Angie?" David stopped chewing his bite of toast and looked at Maddy.

"Where did you hear that name?" he asked with a look of surprise.

"You were talking in your sleep just before the crash of thunder that woke us up," Maddy answered.

"I guess I must have been dreaming, but I don't remember what the dream was about," he said.

"Maybe you dreamt that a pack of hyenas were attacking Angie and you killed the wild beasts," she answered.

The two of them got into the ATV and drove out of the ranch yard and onto a field of plants. The plants had a unique flower on top and leaves like some of the herb plants that David had planted in Helen's and his garden in Minnesota. "Stop, I would like to pick a couple of the plants," David said. He walked over to the field of plants, pulled up two plants including the roots, and walked back to the ATV. "Have you ever made tea from the dried flowers?' David asked curiously.

"No, I have not," Maddy answered with a smile. "Maybe I should. We may develop a new product." They drove the ATV over to the shed. "This is where the crop is being dried, boxed, and stored for shipment. "I don't think anyone is here and I do not have a key." David thought about his ability to access most buildings and their doorways. He had learned much of this ability in Agency training and at his home in Minnesota.

"Maybe there is an open door or window," David said. "I'm going to look around."

"I think everything is locked up tight, Alex," Maddy responded with a voice of hesitation. He circled the shed while she followed behind him. Soon he tried a door on the opposite side of the building and found it was unlocked. He walked inside. The first thing that David noticed gave him the positive conclusion that the entire operation was where all of the illegal dope was being processed. He could smell it. In a cabinet on the wall were the names and addresses of some of the more famous drug dealers in the west. David recognized many of the names. He read the list again and memorized any unfamiliar names. Suddenly Dave received a buzz on his phone. It was from the Agency.

"David, you have only one hour to get out of there. Maddy's mother and dad are about to arrive at the ranch. They have with them a hit man who is contracted to kill both parents and their daughter."

"I'll see what I can do to save all of them," David said in a whispered voice that Maddy could not hear.

Within an hour a plane could be heard in the skies above. It contained a pilot, Maddy's parents, and the man who was supposedly the hit man from whatever organization had contracted him. David and Maddy ran out to the runway near the ranch pasture where the beef herd was grazing.

When the plane landed Maddy ran to greet her parents as they exited the plane. David was introduced to her mom and dad. They all went immediately to the weed processing shed. David quickly corralled the family and spoke to them. The hit man suddenly walked back to inside the plane, maybe to get his weapon. "I need to get you folks and Maddy away from here," David whispered. "Trust me. You are all about to be shot. Quickly, jump onto this ATV. I will get you to safety."

# Chapter 5

David drove the ATV down the road and into the jungle to where his car was parked. He drove as fast as he dared. The ATV was very crowded. "OK, everyone into the car." For some reason they all did what he asked with no argument or discussion. They all exited off of the vehicle and entered the car. David parked the ATV in some jungle thicket and jumped into the car himself. He maneuvered the car out onto the road and took off. No one said a thing until they were well out of where the jungle was the thickest. "OK everybody, my name is David." Maddy quickly turned to him.

"You told me your name was Alex," Maddy retorted with a sense of distrust. "What else did you tell me that wasn't the truth?"

"I will tell you later, Maddy. Right now we need to drive to a safe place." Maddy's mother and Dad were wondering what exactly was going on with their daughter and this strange young man. Within 30 minutes David drove into a driveway, to behind a small grove of trees and out of sight from the road. He stopped the car and turned off the motor.

"Can we all get out of the car now?" Maddy asked.

"Please do," David answered. He took a deep breath as he shut the car door. There happened to be two tree logs next to each other where they had stopped. "Let's sit on these logs and I will tell you what the excitement is all about."

"I wish you would," Maddy's father replied with a noticeable sense of irritation. David started to explain.

"I work for a medical company in the Washington, DC area. We are looking for new plants which may contain elements that may be the next great medical cure—the one that contains the cure for some incurable infections or diseases. I have some samples that I picked out of one of your fields. I will bring them to a lab location for a close scientific study." David was not telling them the real reason for his presence in Kenya. His audience never suspected that he was not telling them the whole truth—except for maybe Maddy.

"What was the reason you told us that someone was about to kill us?" Maddy's dad asked David.

"Just prior to your landing at the runway my company called me and said that you were coming and that some drug man was also flying in on the same plane and planned to kill all three of you." David didn't wish to answer any additional questions, but he was ready just in case.

"How did your company know us and that we were flying into our airport?" Maddy's mother asked. David had to come up with a satisfactory answer quickly. "That guy did look a little suspicious, to tell the truth."

"My company knows about your operation. That is all I know." David told them about Maddy picking him up along the road and providing a place to stay. "By the way folks, my company is sending a check to you for my stay at your ranch." David was careful how he worded his answers so as not to get Maddy in trouble. Her parents had looked at Maddy with a questioning eye, which David noticed.

"Now what do we do, David?" Maddy's father asked. "And, who are these thugs that are trying to kill us?" David thought for a few seconds. *How should I answer that question? If I say too much I will be telling Maddy that her parents are unknowingly mixed up with a drug cartel.*

"To tell the truth, I do not know the answer to that question. I can only think of a couple possibilities."

"Tell me what those are," Maddy's father said, in a manner that showed that he seemed worried of what David knew.

"One possibility is that it is someone who is attempting to get at your property because of what may be in the ground—minerals. The other is that a terrorist group located close by is attempting to gain a foothold in this area of Kenya." The answer was good enough for Maddy's parents so that they decided to not ask any more questions.

"Now, what are we going to do or where are we going?" Maddy's mother asked.

"What I will do is to take you folks into Nairobi, drop you off at a motel, and continue on my journey. I will then take Maddy to wherever she wishes to go or she can stay with you." David was very sure that Maddy was working for the Agency or had been contracted by the Agency to work on this particular project with him.

After David dropped off her parents, Maddy turned to David and said, "I want to go with you and help you with your work. You may need me." David's suspicion was correct that Maddy was one of two people—*either she is working as another agent, or she is working as a counterspy.* The Agency did not say anything about her occupation, but then again, it was something that was sometimes done to keep the agents secret and in reserve until needed in a particular country. David decided to play along with Maddy.

"That's fine Maddy, as long as you don't interfere with the work that I am doing," David responded.

Maddy transferred to the front seat by David. "We need to find somewhere to sleep tonight," David said. "See if you can find a motel somewhere close by."

"There is the entrance to the Nairobi National Park. I believe that there is a hotel there. It's about 2 hours away from where we are now."

After making their way thru the jungle with many turns, they finally reached the drive-up entrance to the Kenyan Motel. David found a parking place and shut off the motor. David turned to Maddy.

"Let's see if they have 2 single rooms available," David suggested.

"Why not just one room?" Maddy responded in a suggestive manner. "Oh, that's right. You wish to flee from all appearance of evil. I believe that is what you told me when we first met." David never responded. They both exited the car and walked into the motel. Sitting behind the registration desk was a tall bushy haired man with a handlebar mustache. He was busy at his computer and the new guests had to wait about a full minute before getting any response. The man finally pushed himself away from his desk and looked up.

"Can I help you?" he spoke with an English accent.

"Yes," David answered. "We need two rooms."

"I have two single rooms left," he answered. "It is our busy season and we are all filled up. They're yours if you want them. We'll need to clean them up first."

"We'll take'em," David responded without any hesitation. The clerk had David fill out a registration card and gave a key to each of the two new guests. David wrote different names for both Maddy and himself. They were soon at their room door at the end of a hall. Maddy looked at David as soon as he unlocked the door and spoke.

"Have a good sleep David. Don't let the bed bugs bite."

"Don't say that Maddy," David replied, "some of these motels are crawling with them."

At about 4 a.m. David had a call on his secured line. It was his Agency boss. "We need to talk," he said.

"Just a minute," David answered. He walked outside to a spot where no one could possibly hear and where he felt more private. "Ok, talk."

"We have found where the terrorist group is located. It's only a short distance from where you are at now. When you get up in the morning, call us back and we will guide you to the spot."

"I've got Maddy with me," David commented, "What should I do with her?" The agent on the phone paused for a moment.

"Oh, I forgot to tell you," the agent answered, "she is your new partner."

"Gee, thanks. How trustworthy is she? How long has she been an agent?"

"About five years," the agent responded. "She was recruited from where she went to college in the United States. She speaks at least 5 languages. You will need her to translate."

"Ok. I will talk to her when she wakes up. Does she know that I am an agent?"

"I think she suspects that you are." He said. David said good bye and went back to bed. He was now wide awake and sleep was impossible. He could hear and sense that Maddy was stirring also through the thin walls. He got up and went to the bathroom. He could now hear that she was also arising in the room next to his. This particular motel had no eating place connected with it, so the question was: where could the two of them find enough nourishment to last them the day? Just then David's phone beeped.

"Good morning sleepy head!"Maddy said. "Where are we going this morning? Another Jungle area? Or, are we going to find a Perkins restaurant." They both retrieved their gear and got into the car. They would be driving in the dark since it was still early morning.

"Well, maybe we should pray for a food miracle from God." David suggested, knowing that Maddy may not appreciate any mention of God.

"Whatever," Maddy answered in a knowingly mocking manner. David immediately begin to pray out loud.

*"Lord, we are hungry and need something to eat. Provide us with some of your creation in the form of edible food."* In the next two miles David noticed something growing alongside the road. The headlights provided enough light to see them. He quickly stopped and jumped out of the car. Soon he came back with two handfuls of avocados and wild gooseberries.

"What have you got, David?" Maddy asked, "something to eat?"

"In my country, what I have in my hands would be called edible fruit." David responded. They both started to eat. They were hungry, and since there were no eating places where they were headed, they needed to eat as much as possible. Maddy opened the car door and picked some more fruit. When they had eaten all of what they had picked, they both exited the car and picked more fruit for a future meal, placing them in an empty cardboard box that was on the backseat. Soon they were on their way again.

"So, David, where are we headed?" Maddy asked. David wasn't sure and needed some direction from the Agency. His boss had told him that Maddy was also an agent and he needed to discuss with her the ground rules for their working relationship. Of most importance was the need for David to make her understand that she needed to be completely honest with him.

"Maddy, since you are also an agent, we need to begin cooperating and trusting each other. We are headed to an area where a drug cartel is headquartered. Our task is to disrupt and destroy as much of their operation as possible." She did not act surprised when David revealed that they were both agents.

"Do you have any ideas of how we are to do that?" Maddy asked."

"No, I do not know, but we can work together to figure it out. The first thing we need to do is to secure aerial photographs of their place of operation. The agency is sending what photos they have. It's up to us to formulate a plan of attack."

"Do the thugs have any idea that we are in route to their campsite?"

*The Garden*

"I don't think so, Maddy, and that is where we have an advantage. However, they probably possess similar surveillance techniques and equipment that we have."

Within 20 minutes the G.P.S. indicated the two agents were within a 2-mile range of where the camp was. David found what looked like a road into the forest. He slowly turned into it and drove until he was well out of sight from the road. "It's too early to be able to see what we are doing," David whispered, "so let's explore the area within a few hundred feet of the car. Keep your eyes and ears open for anything that is interesting. And, let's be careful that we do not get lost."

"Maybe we can find some more fruit. Should I taste anything I find?" Maddy asked.

"I wouldn't do that, if you're smart." David answered.

"OK, chief." Maddy replied. From that answer she let David know that he was her superior in this agent/agent relationship. This fact was important. Although independence was an important element with the Agency, working together took priority.

They both spent the next half hour combing the area around them and then returning with nothing unusual to report. They decided to relax inside the car.

They both were startled by a strange noise at about 5:30 am. The noise was just outside the car. David pulled out his gun in one hand and his flashlight in the other and slowly opened the car door. There, about 50 feet from the car was a parachute with a package tied to it. "Maddy, are you awake? Let's go have some breakfast."

"OK," answered Maddy, "but first I need to go to the bathroom."

"I will walk over to the parachute," David said, "while you go behind the car. Take your gun with you." Maddy found a bush where she would be shielded from any intruders—be they the

## The Garden

human kind or animals. She had gone to the bathroom in the jungle several times before. The one thing she always feared was if a snake or lizard made her a target as she was doing her business. She returned to the car where David was in the process of eating from a box of rations. Orange juice completed the meal.

"I asked the blessing on the food for both of us," David said.

"Thank you David," Maddy answered in a cynical manner. David just smiled. Just then, David had a signal that he was to communicate with his boss. No longer was he needing to shield Maddy from any communique. She was now his partner.

"What's up?" David asked of his boss.

"We have information that a shipment of the hard stuff is about to arrive only 2 miles from where you are at the present time. It needs to be destroyed. See if you and Maddy can get close enough to place explosive devices on their vehicles. But, be careful. Oh, and one other thing—their processing plant is underground. Find it and blow it to smithereens." No more was said and both David and Maddy prepared to walk to where the drug camp was located.

David and Maddy pushed the car under a bush that covered it almost completely. They strapped on two guns each and made sure they were fully loaded and ready to shoot. They also had several clips of ammo strapped on their belts in case they needed them. In two small canvas bags were 4 plastic explosives each. They began to walk toward where their G.P.S. indicated. They suspected that the forest was bugged so they did not talk—only mouthed words and used hand signals. The forest was thick and Maddy was having a little trouble where it contained a thick underbrush. "Let's stop and rest a while," David mouthed to Maddy.

"Thank you, David," she mouthed back with a sigh, "you are so kind." They found a couple of rocks next to each other made to order for two people to sit.

Suddenly they stopped abruptly and looked at each other. The early morning jungle stillness permitted the two agents to feel a sudden jolt of activity. They felt the earth vibrate. David placed his mouth next to Maddy's ear. "That noise was a truck

*The Garden*

moving. I think they are loading a truck, probably with the drugs. Let's see if we can get close to it and place the explosives on the truck."

"We need to hurry," Maddy spoke very quietly back in David's ear, "because the sun is about to come up and we will be easily spotted, especially here in Kenya." Suddenly they both heard a door slam. They moved closer and could see the backup red lights on the truck through the dense jungle growth. They motioned to each other to move quickly to each side of the truck and place the explosive charges on either side. Their task would then be completed, if the explosives detonated. There was plenty of brush cover to hide both of them from being seen by the people in the truck. It took less than a minute to place the explosives under the truck next to the gas tank. They also placed an explosive charge in back of a car that accompanied the truck. 3 people were in the car and 2 people were in the truck.

They quickly hid in the dense forest. Within 2 minutes the truck was on the main road to wherever it was going. There were four sudden explosions a few seconds apart followed by the explosion of the car. The sky lit up with fire. "What's next, David," Maddy asked?

"We need to blow up the underground processing operation by throwing explosives into the basement." They quickly found the trap doors for the basement factory, threw down two explosives in each one, and ran toward where their car was parked. Almost immediately, the ground shook. David once again had mixed feelings about what he and his partner had just done—caused the death of an undetermined number of people. On the other hand, by doing so they may have elimated an undetermined number of deaths from the effects of drugs. It was the tradeoff that agents faced in their work.

Maddy and David quickly drove toward the ranch once again. After a few miles he received a message from the Agency office." You are to be congratulated on the job well done in destroying

## The Garden

the drugs and their manufacturing facility." David thought for a moment. He had just been a participant in destroying many lives and hundreds of pounds of destructive drugs. His thoughts continued back to when he was in the Agency training group. He questioned whether he should be in such a career that resulted in deaths of people even though they were depraved characters. He finally developed an attitude that gave him the rationalization he was looking for. He told it to his Agency class and teacher.

"We are in the business of preventing deaths and suffering. If we can stop the drug flow, then maybe it will save some kids from death. If we can eliminate the drug traffickers, the same may result. God will judge the drug supplier, the drug consumer, and the person who stops them. He will be a just Judge."

"Where do we go next, sir?" David asked the Agency operator.

"Actually, both you and Maddy need to return to the ranch to do some cleanup."

"Exactly what do you mean by cleanup?" David asked.

"A crew from the Agency raiding the Ranch using metal detectors found drugs of many kinds buried in the ground in some kind of metal containers. Someone did this. This fact is known only by our Agency and we need someone who is trustworthy to find the loot and burn them before the word gets around."

"How soon can we get there and start?" David asked.

"As fast as you can drive," was the answer. David turned off his phone and drove as fast as allowed toward the ranch. Maddy had her electronic device with her that opened the front gate lock. When they arrived, there was no one at the ranch. Since David did not let Maddy hear what the Agency had told him about the hidden drugs, he wondered if she was privy to this information from before. Maybe she or her family had hidden the drugs. If there was a chance that she had knowledge of this underground stockpile, then how should he handle the demolition task? He needed to talk to the Agency concerning this manner.

He went for a short walk in back of the big barn while Maddy fixed some lunch for the two of them. The ranch chef was gone also. David called the Agency to voice his concern of Maddy's commitment in the demolition of the drugs.

## The Garden

"We never thought of that. You handle it in the best way you can," the Agency person on the phone said. "If you think that it is going to be a problem, let us know. We will take her out of there before you begin."

David walked into the barn through the same unlocked door that he entered before. He went to a room that looked like an office and broke in. There was a desk that had a bunch of papers in it that contained various relevant information. Just when he was about to leave, he spotted a map of the ranch. It had places marked with distances to trees, buildings, big rocks, and fences. It was the map of where the drugs were buried. They were in steel containers so that they would be sealed from the moisture and would insure their freshness. There were 11 places listed with the name of the drug contained therein: meth, lsd, pcp, psilocybin mushrooms, cocaine, marijuana, opium, ecstasy, crack cocaine and heroin. Whoever obtained these drugs went through a lot of work to collect them and bury them. David's answer to whether or not Maddy could be trusted to help him dig them up and destroy them still was not answered.

He went back to the ranch house where Maddy was preparing a lunch. She was about to serve the lunch on the patio table under an oak tree. "Maddy, please excuse me while I go wash my hands."

"Please take your time." She answered. He walked inside and found Maddy's purse. Her gun was at the bottom and he took the bullets out. Then he ran to the bathroom off of the kitchen and washed his hands.

"The lunch looks great, Maddy, thank you." They spent the next 15 minutes eating and enjoying the hot sun and the jungle sounds. "Maddy, I found a map in the big barn with 11 spots where drugs are supposedly buried." As he spoke these words, David looked deep into her eyes. He saw a reaction that told him that she knew about them and what she was planning to do.

"What kind of drugs?" she asked.

"11 different drugs. This is our next task—to dig them up and destroy them." They quickly finished their lunch and headed outside. Maddy stopped.

"I need to get my purse. I will catch up to you." David imagined in his mind where she walked to get her purse. His timing never had time for her to check the gun inside. *She has to know that gun is loaded,* he thought to himself. Soon she returned. "So, when we dig all of these drugs up, what will we do with them?"

"Let's find the first one to make sure that the map is accurate," David replied. He took the drug map out of his pocket and walked to where a container of opium was supposedly buried. It was 3 feet from the edge of a flower garden that Maddy's mother had planted. Maddy dug with a shovel that they brought with them. After digging a hole 12 inches deep, they heard a 'clunk' sound. "That is one of them," David exclaimed with a note of excitement. "Ok, let's empty out the contents and destroy the opium."

"Why don't we wait until we have them all in a pile? Then we will build a big fire and burn them all at one time." David was waiting for that exact question from Maddy.

"Here is the answer to that question," he answered knowing what she was up to. "Both of us know the value of the drugs we are digging up. And, we both could get rich if we sold them, depending on whether they are still fresh. It would be tempting to do such a thing. You don't fully know me and I don't fully know you. So, to keep such a thing from happening, we need to burn the drugs as we dig them?" Maddy was quiet for a moment. All she could think of was the money she could acquire from selling the drugs. She reached for her purse. David knew what would happen next. "Here are the bullets for your gun. Just leave the gun where it is at. Make your parents proud of you and preserve your good record with the Agency. Put evil out of your thinking and let's get this job done." She stood straight up, dropping her purse back to the ground, and stood with an ashamed look on her face.

"I'm sorry David," she said as she grabbed her shovel and continued working. "I am not thinking. It's just that my parents are about to lose this farm leaving me with nothing. Also, we do not get paid that well working for the Agency."

"Maddy, you are young and you can acquire your own wealth," David countered her selfish reason for her wanting to do wrong.

They were soon back at work digging up the containers, emptying them on the ground, and burning the steel container contents—one by one. Some of the drugs needed to be burned away from the two Agency partners so as not to expose them to the effects of the drug fumes. When they completed their task they were both tired. They buried the steel containers back into the hole from which they came. This was in case the people who buried them might come back for them. The Agency would then have a way to apprehend the culprits.

"We are done with destroying the drugs." David told his Agency supervisor on the phone. "But why did you have us bury the steel drum back in the ground?"

"We will have a G.P.S signal pointed on them. There may be many people who have knowledge of these hidden drums and what is inside of them. Soon we will place a camera close by. Perhaps we will catch a bunch of drug dealers there."

When they were done destroying the drugs, Maddy was told to come back to the Agency headquarters. Before she left on a helicopter, she had a request for David.

"David," she said in a somber voice, "would you please pray for me from time to time?"

David looked at her, grabbed her and gave her a slight hug.

"Maddy," he responded, "I will do that if you promise me something."

"What is that?" she asked.

"You have listened to me pray. Now you can pray for yourself. OK?"

"OK David." Then Maddy boarded the helicopter.

It was time for David to take some more vacation. He had thought about two choices—either a relaxing trip to Florida or back home in Minnesota to work on the garden. He had acquired some seeds from Africa and wanted to see if they would grow in Northern Minnesota. He finally decided on the latter option. Another reason for his choice was he desired to see how his boyhood friend Angie was getting along. As far as he knew she was still in drug rehab in Saint Paul. This time his trip to Minnesota would not include a stop to see her. He could find out from his dad and Helen exactly how she was getting along.

He boarded an airline from Nairobi to Addis Abba, Ethiopia. From there he flew to Frankfurt, Germany. He had a 12 hour layover at the airport in Frankfurt and was to meet with a fellow Agent to review some cases in various parts of the world. The agent was one of his trainers in Agency school, James Frisk. James was also a medical doctor. They were to meet at the McDonalds at the Frankfurt airport at 10 pm. They were both able to pass through security without any problem.

"James," David called out when he got to the line and saw his friend. "How are you?"

"David, it is good to see you once again." James looked like a medical doctor which was a good cover for his new second profession. He had served as a surgeon in a Minnesota hospital for 15 years before being recruited by the Agency. Both his father and grandfather had been medical doctors—all three of them at the same medical facility.

"James," David replied, "you were a good instructor and I have used your teaching and knowledge many times in my cases."

"Thank you for the compliment David: you were a good student." They both ordered some food and found a secure place to eat and visit. Since both David and James were known to some of the drug cartels and industrial spies in the world, there was a good chance there might be someone or some recording device that would be where they may be most likely to sit. James had taken care of that prior to their meeting.

"What's new, James?" David asked with his small notebook ready to record the latest Agency happenings.

"About the same turmoil as before," James answered. "Greed and sin don't change much, only the characters."

"James," David said, "did you ever have a course on dreams or subconscious visions in your medical training?"

*The Garden*

"Actually, I did have a course as an elective my final undergraduate school," James answered. "The course was entitld 'Dreams, Visions and Reality.'" He thought it sort of strange that this subject came up between them. "Why do you ask, David?"

"I've told the following to only a couple people in my life: My mother was raped and killed by a homeless guy when I was 4 years old, while I watched. Right after it happened, I begin to experience nighttime visions of this man's face. Then, many years ago I saw what looked like the same individual in the airport in Minneapolis. My mind fixed on this face to the point where it too became an image that my mind occasionally recalls, only the man is 20 or 25 years older. What do you make of this?"

"It sounds like it's the same person."

"That's what I think also, James," David responded. "I believe that God has placed those images in my mind for some future use."

"Let me know if something results from your job and those images. That would make a good story. I will say this—it probably was the result of a traumatic experience."

They spent two more hours chatting about various topics and then relaxed on the terminal benches until their plane departed in the morning.

David rented a car at the Minneapolis airport and continued his week vacation. His trip to northern Minnesota was close to where he had helped a widow and her son to plant a garden the last time he traveled on his way to Dalestown. When he arrived at the small farm he was greeted by the mother. "How are you, David?" the mother greeted. "Since you were here we've talked about you often."

"And I about you, Henrietta." he responded. "I assume that you are still gardening."

"Come and see." The mother took David's hand and walked him back to where he had helped them to plant the garden the last time he was there.

## The Garden

"Where's Jerry?" he asked. David wasn't thinking about it being a school day.

"In school." She answered. "He will be arriving home on a bus in a few minutes."

"I see that the garden is a lot bigger than the one we planted. How is the marketing of the veggies going?"

"Well, I'll tell you. When you were here, I was about to sell the farm. Now I am going to stay. Your help was an inspiration to us."

"That's wonderful. I will stay until Jerry comes home then I need to get going." Just then a big yellow bus pulled up on the road. Jerry immediately saw David as he got off the bus.

"David," he yelled out, "you came back."

"Jerry, your garden looks wonderful," David remarked to Jerry. Henrietta then turned to David.

"The last time you were here, you said that I needed to find a nice single man that could be a father to Jerry, after we got married, that is.

"I remember that," David responded hoping that her next statement would be that she was successful.

"Well, next Saturday, Frank and I will be married in our front yard," Henrietta said.

"That is wonderful," David responded. "I have often prayed for you folks."

"And we have prayed for you too," Henrietta answered.

"Thank you. Your prayers have protected me several times."

Once again David's family in Dalestown was very glad to see him. He would spend the next 2 weeks planting the seeds that he had acquired in various countries. He used the Internet to research each seed to see if it would grow in a northern climate and just exactly how to plant them. Some of the planting information he acquired from friends while on assignment.

Helen was busy working with the garden and let David be undisturbed in his planting. Many of the acquired plant seeds

*The Garden*

were similar to what was grown in the US. Some he had never seen or heard of. He wondered how they would taste if they survived the cool nights in the fall. Along with planting the seeds in the garden, he planted seeds in flower pots in the small heated greenhouse that his father Ralph had built.

"David," Helen asked, "what are you planting now?"

"Along with the vegetable seeds, I brought back some wild flower seeds. I will plant these for Angie in case she comes home. We will call these 10 flower, our African collection."

"That's beautiful, David," Ralph said, "if she comes home and I hope she does."

As his days off came to an end, David received a call from the Agency telling him that a new agent was coming to see him about his next assignment. It was good timing since he was done with the planting of the new and different seeds he had obtained in Africa.

A rental car drove up to the house on a Saturday morning. A young woman exited the car and walked over to where David was working in the garden. "Hi, "she said as she shook David's hand, "my name is Francine. You can call me Fran."

"I am David," he answered. Fran was an attractive young blond haired medium built woman with blue eyes. Her voice had a Scandinavian accent to it. "I will bet that you are from Sweden, aren't you?"

"You guessed it, David." She looked at him for a few seconds and then spoke. "And I think I detect a slight Scandinavian accent in your voice also, David."

"Half Norwegian and half Finnish. So, before we go into the house and talk, let me ask you if you can stay for lunch?"

"I would love to," she answered in an appreciative voice. David took her by the hand and led her into the house.

"Helen, we have a special guest for lunch," he sounded out. Helen had been warned that this could happen.

*The Garden*

"I'm all set David, it's in the oven," she answered. Helen was advised that the two agents needed to talk in private and departed from the house and went into the garden.

"David, "what do you know about human trafficking?" Fran asked. David immediately wondered if this was going to be his next assignment.

"Well," he began to answer, "I do know that it is a multi-million dollar business and is world-wide. I also know that it is spreading fast in this country. Almost every newscast has a story of missing young girls. I also have my own theory of why it's spreading in this country."

"What's that, David?" Fran asked with interest.

"My theory is connected with the breakdown of the home — homes where there is conflict and turmoil producing young girls who are looking for an escape. Some even have no fear of having sex and getting pregnant if it gets them away from all the family conflict. Some will go with any man who wants to take them to Europe. They are prime candidates." Fran seemed very interested in David's comments.

"It sounds like you have a basic understanding of this particular evil." Fran commented. "The Agency is being asked to investigate and try to find some of the missing girls."

After lunch the two agents were on their way to the Minneapolis airport, in their own rental cars, to catch their flight.

# Chapter 6

Both agents were on a plane 24 hours later to a new location. It was on an Agency jet plane and only the pilot knew where it was to land. They both could see that wherever it was, it was not close to a populated area. As they landed David happened to spot a small garden where two people were working. "I will let you off here and here is what I was asked to give you," the pilot announced as he handed David an envelope.

"Thank you," David responded. "So, tell us, where are we?"

"In the country of Iran," the young pilot answered, "far away from populated areas—mostly farmland. There are two people working in a field about a half mile down field. You are to contact them for further instructions." Both Fran and David were surprised. They guessed that they would be going into the African continent. The pilot helped them get their small suitcases out of the baggage compartment and bid them farewell. "We'll probably see you again sometime—keep safe."

They were let off near a 4 foot wide path that started between a corn plot and a plot of squash. It was somewhat difficult to walk because of the uneven ground. David took Fran's hand. "I don't want you to fall, Fran. This is not the easiest or safest ground to walk on."

"Thank you, David," she said in an appreciative manner. "I wish all our male agents were gentlemen." Fran was expecting

*The Garden*

an answer and David couldn't think of one right away. He walked a little further and finally thought of a good answer.

"I believe that if we are nice to people, they maybe will, in turn, pass the kindness on. Also, you and I seem like nice people and deserve all the niceties we can get in our line of work. Our work involves either destroying illegal drugs or leading bad men and women into their destruction so more people will not become addicted or die."

"True, David," Fran responded. "Also passing information that sometimes is not good news."

"Sometimes information that leads to impending destruction and pain," David added. "And, if we don't receive some occasional generosity and love from our fellow man or woman, what will we be like when we retire from our current jobs?"

"Probably bitter old grouches," Fran answered.

"Exactly," David responded. "However, there is another reason why I am like that. I wasn't very nice to the little girls in our neighborhood when I was a little boy. I am making up for past sins."

The two agents kept walking for another mile until they saw the same man and woman working in what looked like a cucumber patch. They both wondered if they would be able to understand the couple's language.

"Hi folks," the woman said to David and Fran. They came together and shook hands all around. "Let us take you to our home where you will stay, and we will discuss what you are to do." The four of them walked for another 500 feet until they came to a small structure with a flat roof. Right beside the home was another small building where there were containers of plants just starting to grow and sitting on racks. David recognized most of the plants except for a few of them. He figured that they were native to this region or to the Iranian culture cuisine. The two hosts did not say anything until they stepped inside the home. "David, you can sleep up in the loft and Fran, you may use our guest bedroom." Fran and David looked at each other in surprise when the husband said their name.

*The Garden*

"Thank you very much for welcoming us as guests into your home," David said in appreciation. "I assume that you are going to inform us of our mission here."

"Yes, indeed," he answered. The man's English was impeccable. "We will talk about it during dinner. Maybe Fran could help my wife with dinner and you can help me with some questions that I have about our gardens. After all, you are an expert." David wondered how the man knew that he was a gardener.

"Of course I will." David answered, "But first, I need to know your names."

"Pardon me, we should have introduce ourselves when you first landed. My name is Amir, which is a Farsi name and means King Emir, after one of the early kings of this region. My wife's name is Parto, which is also Farsi and means 'rays of light'."

"You and your wife speak very good English," David commented. "Where did you learn it?"

"Our parents sent us to school in America from the 8th grade thru college," Parto answered. "We made it our goal to be able to speak perfect English."

"You surely succeeded in accomplishing that goal," Fran responded. "Those are interesting names. You must tell us about your background while we are here." The two men departed from the women and disappeared into a field which contained a series of garden plots.

"Let me show you my squash plots which I just planted. We have never had a crop that the squash larvae did not destroy. Maybe you have the answer." David had a slight smile on his face as he listened carefully to Amir explain his plight with the squash. It was like David's experience back in Minnesota with the same squash larvae.

"Well Mr. Amir," David responded with much interest, "it appears that you and I have the same difficulty. Here is what I have tried. I try to grow a type of squash that has a tough stem. The squash larva moth plants her eggs in the dirt where and when the plant emerges out of the ground. I have had some success with wrapping aluminum foil around the stem. Then, I dust the ground with a product that will kill or inhibit the mother moth from laying her eggs or kill the larvae when they hatch." Amir stood by the plot taking notes with a pencil and paper.

"I will try it," Amir responded.

"Once the mama moth's eggs hatch, the larvae will bore inside the stem and eat their way up the plant. They will eat and poop and will eventually kill the plant."

"That is exactly what happens to the plants," Amir added with a slight laugh.

"Also, you might try another method in addition to what I have mentioned," David added. "Try growing a variety of different squash, if you have the seeds, planting them in different spots. What you do is to fool the mama moth. She thinks she is done laying eggs for the year. She may not have the energy to look for other squash seed locations."

"David, you are a genius. I will let you know how it works out."

"Amir, why are Fran and I here in Iran?" David walked over to a 5 gallon bucket and sat down on it. Amir joined him on another bucket and they faced each other.

"Here are the two things that the agency wants done." Amir sat quietly for a few seconds as he seemed to struggle with the correct words to use. "First of all, there is a gang of drug dealers who are wanting to introduce a new drug into the United States. It's a mixture between cocaine and a new weed, the result which is really bad news. We need to find out about it, do what we can to stop its growth, and its transport." David was ready with a question.

"So how are we supposed to destroy it?

"Here is the big challenge," Amir responded, "The people who are behind this drug business are using stuffed birds from Kenya to smuggle the drug into the United States." David sat still for a few seconds wondering if his next life threatening experience was going to be inspecting stuffed birds from the continent of Africa. Fran suddenly joined them in their discussion.

"So, Amir, do the Kenyan birds have secret pockets where they hide the drug as they go through customs." Amir broke out with a quiet laugh.

*The Garden*

"How in the world are they stuffing the birds with drugs?" David inquired with an expression of doubt.

"That is our challenge, David," Fran responded, "Where are they hiding the drugs inside the animals? Or, are the drugs being hidden in the packaging that houses the birds as they travel to the United States?"

"What birds are we talking about?" David asked.

"Various birds that are about the same size," Amir slowly answered. "The drug people try to use birds that are not too big, but big enough to pack inside a good quantity of the drug. They want to use the same size carton. What disturbs us most is that they trap or capture certain birds and then kill them with poison. They like to find birds that are about to lay their eggs. That way they think that the inside of the bird is as big as possible prior to killing and stuffing them with a plastic bag full of the drug."

"That is horrible," David commented. "Those people need to be stuffed. So what is the other project that the Agency has up their sleeve for us?"

"It involves the plants and seeds that you brought with you from Kenya. You and I are to plant them and the seeds in various plots. I will cultivate them, harvest them, and report the results."

Amir's wife soon called for the men to gather around the table for dinner. Everyone was hungry. Fran and David were anticipating a unique meal that Amir's wife Parto had been preparing for her guests.

"The dinner that you have prepared looks and smells wonderful," David said as the various dishes were set on the table. "What are they?"

"They are all Iranian cuisine," Parto responded, "We serve them to all our guests."

Fran and David slept in separate quarters, with respect to David's wishes. Their guests had been advised of this desire of David's from the Agency. During the night, both of the guests

## The Garden

had trouble sleeping and appeared together by the garden at about 2 am. "Fran," David inquired, "you can't sleep either?"

"I cannot," she responded. "It's probably jet lag. Let's share our thoughts. Maybe we'll get tired. I am troubled by the thought of interacting with the drug hoodlums that we will encounter in this assignment." David stopped for a brief moment and just peered at the full moon hoping Fran would get her mind back into sleep.

"Can you believe this, Fran?"

"What?" she responded, "believe what?"

"This beautiful night," David answered: The moon is full, the chorus of insect and small creatures are singing their songs, and the soft breeze is whistling in the garden's growth. I thought that this happened only in Northern Minnesota during the summer."

"It is truly a perfect early morning. I just wish we could take it back with us to the United States," Fran responded in a voice of wishful thinking.

Suddenly Amir appeared in the same garden.

"What's up Amir?" David asked.

"My alarm just sounded." Amir said as he looked into the darkness in back of his house.

"What alarm is that?" David asked.

"My land is surrounded by an electrical wire alarm system. It lets me know when something gets close to it. It could be a furry animal, a big snake, or a human kind of animal." Just then both Amir and David's phone rang softly. They both answered. It was their Agency's boss.

"You've got company, according to our satellite monitor," the voice on both phone calls said. "Get your guns out. I think it's some drug people." Amir stood there while David and Fran, guns drawn, moved to the side and around in back of the garden some 200 feet away, ready for whoever and how many it was. They got down and crawled until they could see two men and a woman in the full moon walking toward the garden in an open field. They too, had guns.

David got close to the men and shouted, "Ok, hold it right there you two and drop those guns." He was directly behind the

*The Garden*

men and was ready to shoot if they even turned around. The woman suddenly turned around and ran. She was apparently scared of being killed by David. He watched her run, out of the corner of his eye. Coming toward the woman was Fran with a gun in hand. With one motion, Fran flipped the woman on her back. She was out like a light.

The two men were about to turn on David. As they turned David quickly shot the guns out of their hands, wounding their fingers. Then he hit them on their heads with one motion. "Hey Amir, I got them. Bring your wife here, she will need to give them medical attention. The Agency will want to get some information out of them."

David wondered who these people were. Amir had no idea. "The Agency warned us about them—maybe they know. I will call them back and ask them." David and Amir secured the three gun-toting terrorist's hands and feet with duct tape. The girls then gave them first aid.

"What are we supposed to do with them?" Amir asked.

"I will call the Agency and have a helicopter pick them up. They will want to interrogate them. "Tomorrow morning we need to get started planting a few plots of the weeds and seeds I took from Maddy's ranch. So, we need to hit the hay.

"Hit the what?" Amir asked.

"Get some sleep," David responded.

Everyone was up early, had a good breakfast and were ready to go to work. "The work of planting the crop of the new weed will not be too difficult, except for building of 4 raised beds," Amir said. "It is something new for us to plant on a raised bed. How do we do it?"

"First we need some materials with which to build it." David said, hoping Amir had some 4 X 4s and some 2 inch wood.

"Well, I think we may be in luck." Amir responded. "There is an old building about a mile from here that the Iranian government was intending to wreck. They came to me and asked if I would do the honors, and take whatever materials I could use."

"Let's go have a look." David answered. "Maybe there will even be some stainless steel screws that we will need." Amir and David walked about 2 blocks to an old warehouse building. From the looks of the outside, it appeared that the building was well-built. They went inside. It was dark until they opened two other doors. "I see right away some 4 X 4s that we can use. Now let's see if we can find some 2 inch thick wood.

"Hey, look over there," exclaimed Amir, "someone has built some raised beds for us."

"Have you a trailer that we can use to haul them to your place?" David asked.

"I do," Amir replied, "and it looks like we can stack them when we haul them."

Soon the beds were sitting in a neat row on the east side of Amir's house. They were three foot in height. "Now what do we do?" Amir asked.

"Do you have any compost or organic material which will turn into compost in 2 years or less?" David asked. Before David finished his question, Amir began walking toward an area where a large pile of animal manure had been sitting for a couple of years. David followed Amir.

"This stuff has been collected from 5 different animals: sheep, cattle, horses, goats, and hogs. I have a screen that we can use to break it up."

"When we are done filling the raised beds," David continued his instruction, "we will place 5 inches of some of your best soil on the top."

The project took the entire day and both men were completely exhausted when done. The two agents/gardeners visited and discussed many subjects during their time together—subjects like politics, family, their work with the Agency, and their lives after they retire from spying.

## The Garden

After both Amir and David had taken their showers from the sticky compost, the two agent couples ended up visiting on a sofa in Amir's living room. They all knew that coffee would keep them awake, so the hosts made some Iranian Tea. "It seems to soothe me," Fran began the late night talk, "sometimes I drink too much coffee. My coffee habit began when I was a teenager back in Sweden."

"My habit began in Minnesota from my Norwegian father," David responded.

"Change of subject," Fran suggested. "What do you people plan to do when you retire from the Agency?" David was asked this question by many people, mostly by the Agency women. It seemed that the women agents were looking for a future spouse. All of Agency men and women were not allowed to be married for security reasons. David's answers to this question were usually somewhat different depending on who the person asking the question was.

"To be honest with you, I want to get married and live in the quiet countryside," David answered. "However, I will need to find another vocation. That will be up to God to decide."

"That is a strange answer, David," Fran responded. "I thought it would be up to you." David was ready for this challenging comment.

"Well Fran," David said, "I don't always choose wisely. I would rather have a wise person choose."

"So who do you plan to marry?" Fran asked. "Do you have someone picked out or do you let God do that, too." David sensing the mocking tone to her voice—he just smiled at her. At this point it seemed that Amir and Parto were being left out of the conversation.

"How about you Fran," David asked with sincere interest. "What are your plans when you decide that you've had enough of the Agency?" She looked at David realizing that her previous comment about God had been cruel and maybe even hurtful.

"Sorry about my comment about God. I was not thinking about what I said. About your question—I have an answer. I plan to get married, if and when I find the right person." David

*The Garden*

thought about her answer and knew what the next logically question should be.

"So tell me, if I may invade your deep thoughts, who would be Mr. Right for you? What would be his personal and physical characteristics?" Fran looked down at her tea cup for the next 15 seconds. Then she looked back up and answered.

"My ideal man would be a carbon copy of my grandpa back in Sweden. He was a loving hardworking thoughtful man who married a beautiful gracious young woman and fathered 6 little Swedish children."

"He sounds like an ideal mate for your grandmother," David responded."

"One other thing that you may be interested in. I know from talking to other agents that you are of the same spirituality as grandpa—both Godly men." David closed his eyes and didn't say a thing.

The next morning the men and women were up early. Amir's wife fixed breakfast while Amir wandered out in the garden thinking of how exactly they were going to plant the seeds of the newly found drug weed in the raised beds. The breakfast consisted of Iranian pancakes, bacon, a mid-eastern omelet, and orange juice. The aroma made its way throughout the house and it succeeded in waking up the two guest agents.

Morning and the sunrise had seemed to come early for the two agent partners. They had finally fallen asleep after a restless night. Their hosts had breakfast ready for them when they appeared in the kitchen, coming at the same time from the two sleeping quarters—Fran from a comfortable small bedroom and David from a crowded upstairs loft with a thin mattress. Their morning meal was sitting on the table. Their host soon came into the house through the front door. "Good morning," Amir said to his guests. "Are you all set to go to work?" Fran and David looked at each other for a moment, both wondering what work he was talking about.

## The Garden

"We are all set to go to work. Can we help you with anything?" David asked.

"As a matter a fact, you can. I need your expertise in applying compost on the garden. I will show you after we finish breakfast." The two men were soon out in back of the house looking at a compost pile.

"What is in this compost pile?" David asked Amir.

"This compost is made up of grass clippings, vegetable peelings from the kitchen, some of the manure from my sheep and lambs, and coffee grounds from my wife's kitchen." Amir looked at David for some look of approval. David responded.

"I'd say that you have a good mixture. But before you dump it on the area that you wish to plant, let's screen the compost." Amir had built a 36" X 36" screen with 1/2 inch spacing the week before. David placed the screen on a barrel and picked up some handfuls of compost and placed on a screen. Using a pair of gloves, he worked the compost mixture back and forth on the screen. Most of the compost filtered right out of the bottom of the screen all broken up. The rest was dumped back onto a new pile of compost. As they were screening, a toy soldier appeared on the screen.

Amir and Parto saw the toy and recognized it immediately. "That belongs to a neighbor's child who I took care of one afternoon a while back," she indicated.

The remainder of the morning was spent getting briefed by Amir on what to look for when investigating the stuffed bird drug smugglers. At about 3 pm all four agents had some Iranian tea and berry pie. They knew it was time to say goodbye when they all heard a small plane once again land on a close by airfield. At the same time David received a message from his agency, "David, we have sent a plane to pick up Fran and you. You and she will each go on the same new assignment."

After the meal, David called into the Agency to obtain the latest update on any fast breaking world spy news. David was told that they would be going on a mission to destroy some drugs. He immediately informed Amir and Fran of the change of plans. "We will be on a helicopter this afternoon traveling to an undisclosed location where we have a task to accomplish."

David and Fran were on their way to the state of Hawaii. Neither of them had been to any of the islands. They traveled through Frankfort, New York, Denver, and on to Honolulu. When they arrived at the airport they were met by two other agents and were immediately ushered into a secure airport room for a meeting. The head of the Hawaii branch of the Agency, Dennis Arneson led the meeting. "Welcome to Hawaii," he announced. "We are here to perform the task of stopping the flow of a certain drug and to assist in the arrest of those people involved with its flow. We will divide you 4 agents into 2 teams—David and Fran, and Warren and Nicole. Any objections to those combinations?"

"Not really chief," David answered. "Only what are we going to be doing and will we have time to do some swimming on Waikiki beach?" There was a slight giggle from the gathered group of agents.

"Don't worry, we'll have some time for that later. Here is the situation. You most likely have heard of the opium trade originating from the Far East involving the countries of Laos, Thailand, Cambodia, and Viet Nam."

"Yes we have," they all answered almost in unison.

"Opium. Opium from the far east," Dennis said. "When some of the refugees came over from the Far East in the 1970s and 1980s, some of the older people came with an acquired habit of using opium. Many of these people had worked in the opium fields in their native country. Of course, the habit continued over at their new homes in the United States. Soon little old grandmas and grandpa began to receive small packages from their homes back in Viet Nam, Laos, Cambodia, and Thailand. Next thing you know, the drug police were showing up at the homes of grandma in Saint Paul, Minnesota, Modest, California, and many other cities, arresting them for possessing opium and even selling it. There were even reports of a General of the

*The Garden*

Laotian army who was running a drug ring using established routes of flights during the Viet Nam war and was continuing it after the war was over. Now we have a new war—second generation ethnic peoples on drugs. Then there was this article in the Christian Science Monitor In 1987." The chief turned on the projector and showed the news clip on the screen:

*Hmong Carry Opium Habits To Their New Life In America.*

*US CATCHES ON SAN DIEGO— Last spring United States postal officials here received an unusual letter. It warned them that ``hundreds and hundreds of opium boxes" were being shipped into California right under their noses. The arrival of the letter coincided with the discovery by drug-sniffing US Customs dogs in Hawaii of opium-stuffed parcels destined for members of the Hmong community here and in other California locations.*

"I heard about this. So what is the fuss about it now?" David inquired?

"The use of this drug has now been acquired by the second and third generation of Hmong people," Dennis replied. "The same routes in which the opium traveled from the opium fields in Laos and Viet Nam have been passed on to the second and third generation of drug dealers and users."

"So, now I suppose that there is an addiction of opium that has resulted in the many cities in the United States," David commented.

"Not only the US, but also in Europe," the head of the Hawaii Agency added. At that point, Dennis was ready to present the group with the next Agency task. "To add fuel to the fire, a group of Hmong are growing the opium somewhere here on this island. They sell the opium to a drug gang and they market it on the island."

"So how can we stop this drug flow?" Fran asked.

"In two ways," Dennis responded. "We need to destroy the opium fields and the processed opium in the producing countries and to do something with the people who are managing the drug flow." David thought for a moment and produced a doubtful expression.

## The Garden

"This involves taking away the livelihood of the producing families in some countries while eliminating the drug flow people," David commented in verbalizing his thoughts. "However, in the process, look how many lives we can rescue from dying and save those who probably will become addicts."

"That is your next assignment," Dennis continued, "you will be meeting with a couple other agents on the other side of the island for some training and information. Get some swimming done and get rested up. You'll be going to work the first thing in the morning."

David and Fran did just that. They first needed to buy some swimming suits at a shop in Waikiki beach. As they walked around the shop David suddenly stopped, stuck out his arm and quietly halted Fran. "Do you smell that smoke?" Fran sniffed the air a couple of times, then answered.

"Yes, I do," she whispered, "what is it?"

"It is opium smoke in its raw form. It's coming from a room just a few feet away. Let me see if I can find the source. You stay here and I will search." David walked thru a curtain of a dressing room. A man had just tried on a swim suit and was apparently about to leave. He must have decided to smoke some opium first. "Oh, I am sorry, I thought this room was empty."

"I was about to leave," the man spoke nervously.

"Hey, is that opium I smell that you are smoking?" David asked. "My girlfriend and I have been looking for some to buy." The man looked at David while he quickly extinguished his pipe.

"Sorry, I don't have any to spare," the man said. "Maybe you can get some over by the beach. There is where I got this stuff."

"How do I know who is selling it?" David inquired.

"Look for an old Hmong woman from Laos who is wearing a purple stone necklace and a purple bun hat. Just walk up to her and say 'Opium buy.'"

"Thank you," David responded. He exited the dressing room and found Fran by the cash register. They each bought a swimsuit and left the store.

"Did you find out anything in the dressing room?" Fran asked.

"Yes I did," David answered.

*The Garden*

---

Soon they were in their swimsuits. David had a simple one that was very modest. They headed for the shore and found a short Hmong woman who was wearing a purple stone necklace and a purple bun hat. "Hello, ma'am," David greeted. She was about 60 years old and had 3 small children surrounding her—probably her grandchildren.

"Hello," she replied in a very distinct Hmong accent, the same accent that David had witnessed at a Minneapolis farmer's market when he was visiting Angie at the rehab center.

"Opium buy," David said just as he had been instructed. The woman reached down to a woven bag on the ground, quickly looked around like she was expecting someone may be observing her, and pulled out a plain brown paper bag filled with some type of substance.

"Fifty bucks," the woman said as plain as she could voice with her Hmong accent. David handed the woman a fifty dollar bill. Fran was off to the side and quickly used her phone camera to video the transaction.

"Thank you, ma'am," David said. "Let's go Fran." They walked to a close by picnic table and sat down. "We need to find out where she goes or who comes to see her."

Each of the two agents took their turn at swimming at the beach while the other stayed and watched. At about 2 pm a man walked up to the Hmong woman and traded woven purses with her, then left. David guessed that the man was probably an American citizen from what was heard from a distance between the Hmong woman and him. David followed the man while Fran kept watching the woman for any additional interesting activity. The man then walked to a car in the beach parking lot. David quickly took out a magnetic communication chip, ran over, reached under, and placed it under the gas tank on the man's car. He then walked back to where Fran was. "Fran, let's go. We need to follow that car." Both agents changed into their street clothes and were soon on the trail of what they assumed was a member of the opium distribution organization in Hawaii.

"The man will probably pick up more drops from little old ladies on his way to his headquarters," Fran commented.

# The Garden

"Yes, indeed, he probably will," David agreed, "and we need to record where some of these locations are."

By the end of the day the man had apparently completed his rounds and stopped at a warehouse building. David contacted the Agency and reported what had happened that day. "Max," he reported, "you should be able to locate where that warehouse is. I placed a communication chip under the pickup man's gas tank," David said.

"Good work David. How many other cars are parked at the building?" David exited the car and walked around to the front.

"I can see 5 cars including the pickup man's car," David answered.

"Now," Max continued, "place a chip on each of the cars. Then find a motel and get some sleep. We will wake you up when the drug crew is gone. Then you will need to get inside the warehouse and destroy any drugs and any processing equipment."

There was a small motel nearby the warehouse. Interestingly, the same cars that were earlier at the warehouse were soon parked in front of the same motel. David reported this to the Agency and they verified this fact by G.P.S. David and Fran slept in the same room but in separate beds, once again. They decided to sleep in the same motel room to provide protection for each other just in case there was any problems. *Maybe the drug dealers got wind of us trailing them*, David thought.

"David," Fran asked, "how are we going to destroy the opium in that warehouse?"

"Fran," he responded, "I have had the same question on my mind. We can't burn the stuff for fear that we would burn the building down."

*The Garden*

"What if we soak it in some kind of liquid and make it unusable and thus unsalable?" Fran suggested. "Of course we need to see how the stuff is sitting at the warehouse."

"It's only 7 pm," David responded. "Let's break into the warehouse and see what our challenge is. We can eat when we get that done." They both walked over to the warehouse around the corner from the motel armed with their guns, flashlights, a crowbar and rubber gloves. There was a side door with a window about 3 feet away. They tried the door, thinking one of the people involved with the drug smuggling ring may have failed to lock it. No such luck. Their guns were ready to use in case a guard was hiding inside or a guard dog was roaming loose.

"Let's try the window," Fran suggested. "I'll use the crowbar. I see there is no lock mechanism on the inside, so this should be easy."

"Hold it a minute, Fran," David said. "Most likely there are some movement sensors hooked up inside to warn them, or they could have some dogs inside."

"So how do we handle those two possibilities?" Fran asked. "Or do we just take a chance." David thought for a minute, then responded.

"We may have to take a chance." Fran opened the window and crawled in. She unlocked the door and let David in. They spent the next 10 minutes walking around with their flashlights, shining them on all parts of the large room.

"Here it is David," Fran exclaimed, "10 large bags of opium pods"

"I do not see any big dogs and there are not any wires indicating an alarm system," David announced. "I think we should take these bags outside and destroy them."

"Let me go in back of the building and see what is there," Fran suggested. "Let me drag the bags over to the door, they are not very heavy." Fran walked outside and found an open field. She now knew exactly what to do. She went to the car and siphoned out two gallons of gas from their rental car. She had found a rubber hose and a can in a corner of the building. Apparently, the drug thugs had the same idea at one time.

*The Garden*

"Where did you learn to siphon gas, Fran?"

"When I was a kid in Sweden," she responded unashamedly.

"Fran, do you have a match?"

"Yes, I do," Fran answered. David knew that she probably did since he had previously smelled the odor of tobacco on Fran. Now all the bags had been emptied on the ground, soaked with gasoline, and ready to be ignited.

"Get ready to run back to the motel, Fran." David struck the match and lit the stack of opium pods at the end opposite of where the wind was blowing. It didn't take long before the entire pile was on fire. Both agents stayed clear of the smoke trying to keep from getting exposed to whatever effects it may inflict on their senses. They soon were in their motel room and watching out the window at the burning opium. As they were watching, one of the gang ran out of one of the rooms. Soon he rapped on three other doors and their occupants scurried out and toward the warehouse.

"David," Fran shouted, "don't you think we had better drive away from here before the gang suspects us in starting the fire."

"Fran, you are correct. Let's get our bags packed and drive a mile or so from here. We have G.P.S. chips on their cars so we can follow them to wherever they go." They packed up and drove their rental car to a spot about a mile away. They parked and watched the burning opium for 30 minutes. During that time the fire trucks came and tried to put out the fire. As soon as the drug dealers heard the fire sirens, they too took off in their cars like scared rats.

"They are not retrieving their stuff at the motel," Fran said.

"Well, let's break into the rooms and see what we can find." David said. It didn't take long for the agents to find a lot of drug evidence within the four motel rooms. "Let's call the police and drug enforcement agency in Honolulu and let them come and have a looksee."

*The Garden*

The two agents drove back to a different motel and checked in separate rooms. "I am going to find a store to get some batteries," David said. At about 9 pm there was a knock on Fran's door. She got up and grabbed her housecoat and put it on.

"Who is it," she asked.

"Room service," the male answer came back in a somewhat familiar voice to Fran. She reached for her gun and slowly opened the door, leaving the chain lock attached. Standing outside the door carrying a tray was David.

"Room service, Fran," he said.

"Why room service?" Fran asked.

"We had a successful assignment in the opium caper. Let me take you out for dinner. Here is some coffee to get us started."

"Where will we go for dinner?" Fran asked.

"Well, what do you like?" David asked in return.

"I like Italian food," Fran responded in return.

"Actually, it's not my idea. It's Max's suggestion," David said. "I just talked to him. He told me that the agency will pay for it."

The two agents were soon at an Italian restaurant in Honolulu at the center of the seating area. They both ordered spaghetti and meatballs, along with a salad. Also sitting in the restaurant was the Hmong woman who sold the opium to David. She didn't recognize David nor Fran. While they were waiting for their food, David thought he would risk something. He walked over to the Hmong woman and sat down by her. She looked at him and became a little nervous. She no doubt had guilty feelings that she was engaged in an illegal activity. David looked at her with a smile. "Are you growing the opium?" She became even more edgy to the point where she was about to leave. She was inside of the booth and would need to crawl over David if she was going to escape. "Why don't your Hmong people grow vegetables and flowers like the Hong in St. Paul and Minneapolis do and sell them at a farmer's market?"

*The Garden*

"I wish we could do that," she answered, "if only I could talk the other Hmong into doing it."

"What is stopping you?" he asked.

"The rabbits and other rodents always eat the plants before they get full grown." At that point David took out a pen and paper and drew a raised bed.

"Plant your crop on a raised bed and keep the rabbits from eating the plants. I do this in my garden in Minnesota. I have wonderful crops." David saw that the waiter had brought their food on a tray and was ready to serve Fran and him. He walked back to his table leaving the pen and paper with the Hmong woman. "Sorry for the interruption, Fran. That wasn't very nice for me to do that. Maybe the food will make up for that distraction."

As they were about to leave the restaurant, the Hmong woman walked over to their table and placed the paper on the table. David looked at it and smiled.

"Six raised beds," the woman said. "Come help us build them."

"Where do you live?" David asked.

"We live on the north side of the Island," the woman said," There are 8 Hmong families. We are planning to plant new crop of opium. Maybe we can find different crop. Maybe you come help us."

"Give us your address and we will come and see your garden tomorrow morning," David responded. "We will also like to meet the Hmong in your community."

Fran and David drove back to their motel and watched some television for the next two hours. When they finally turned the TV off they talked about what they would do the next day. "We need to try to find where the members of the drug gang went and what they are up to," David suggested.

"It is possible that they are in proximity to where the Hmong have their garden," Fran added. "Thank you for the dinner

*The Garden*

---

tonight. That was fun." At that point she threw her arms around David and kissed him.

"You are welcome, Fran." David responded in a surprising tone of voice.

In the morning the two agents checked out of their separate motel rooms and drove to the address provided by the Hmong woman. It was in a trailer park where 10 other units were located. They found the trailer number where the woman lived. She was outside sitting on a chair waiting for them. With her were 3 other Hmong individuals, most likely also residents of the same trailer park. "Hi," she greeting them. "Let me show you gardens." She walked to an open field where at least 10 plots of field had just been harvested, most likely opium.

As they were standing, looking, and thinking of what could be grown in them, Fran noticed something interesting on the other side of the open field. "David, look at the 4 cars over there. They are the same cars as the ones that were at the motel last night. I'll bet those thugs are negotiating the next crop of opium or other drug crop, as we speak."

"I will call the Agency and tell them," David said.

Soon the police were at the garden and arresting the 4 drug hooligans. Fran and David spent the rest of the day convincing the Hmong to select a variety of vegetables to grow as an alternative crop to sell. Because the Hmong were so cooperative with the police, they did not arrest any of the Hmong for their role in the opium distribution.

# Chapter 7

After his adventure in Hawaii, David bid farewell to Fran at the Honolulu airport. She gave him a hug and boarded a flight to New York. *Fran is a delightful woman and maybe she will find a fine Swedish gentleman to marry someday,* he thought to himself.

David was soon on a flight to Samsun, Turkey, a seaport on the Black sea. After his ride to the north side of the town by cab, he walked to the building where he was told by his Agency boss that the shipment of drug stuffed birds was being stored. There he met his new partner. He couldn't believe his ears when he heard, "David," a voice from behind him call out. He could tell immediately that the voice was that of a woman. He turned around as she continued, "I haven't seen you since we were in training together. How have you been?"

"I have been busy chasing the enemy and trying to shed a few pounds," David answered. He suddenly remembered the woman's name. It was Jennifer from his training class "How have you been?" David continued.

"I have had some really interesting assignments in the past two years," Jennifer answered, "and I have often wondered if you and I would ever be teamed up together. You were a good student in our class"

*The Garden*

"I don't know if that is true," David answered with a casual voice. "I always thought that you and I would someday once again meet up. What we have in common is that we are both Christians. We were the only Christians in our training class at the academy among the 30 men and women. It sure seemed like it, anyway."

"Well," Jennifer added, "we are here and on an assignment that will take us to areas of excitement and adventure that hopefully will end in a successful outcome.

"So Jennifer, how much do you know about these drug stuffed birds? Apparently they are being stored for shipment in this building right in front of us."

"I was told the same thing," she responded. "I was also told that our task was to destroy the entire stock of drug stuffed birds. There is someone within the freight company who is part of the drug organization who we need to watch out for. He is very dangerous and will kill anyone who gets in his way."

"The freight will be loaded on a plane tomorrow," David added. "This does not give us much time to figure out what to do. Are you hungry, Jennifer?"

"I could use some nourishment, yes."

The two agents found a small Turkish café close by the hotel where the agency had reserved a room for each of them. They ordered a small plate each of 5 items, including chopped lamb potato hash, an olive veggie salad, black sea fruit salad, a grape leaf wrapped beef brisket, and a Turkish ice cream delight. They paid with cash so as not to leave a paper trail. They discussed a number of personal topics not related to their work with the agency. Jennifer wanted to ask David a question. "David," she began, "have you ever thought about doing something different?"

"I always think about it. Maybe I will someday," David answered.

"My boyfriend and I would like to get married within the next couple of years. Do you think it is a good idea to do this and still work in the Agency?" she asked David. He suddenly had a grimaced look on his face as he thought Jennifer's question over in his mind.

*The Garden*

"If it were me, I would not," David answered. "There are a number of reason."

"What are some of those reasons David?" she asked.

"I think that the mortality rate of the occupation you and I are in is many times the national average. We also spend much of our time in foreign countries. Being separated from your spouse is not a good thing for your marriage. And the list goes on. You may want to think of changing jobs before you decide to take the plunge."

As they were talking and eating, David suddenly caught a word from the table next to theirs. A man was talking on the phone. David quickly placed his one finger over his closed mouth indicating they needed to be quiet. After a few more seconds David leaned across the table and spoke in a whispered tone.

"Jennifer, someone at the next table just said the word 'feathers' on his phone. That is the code word for the smuggling of the drugs in the birds. When they leave, I will follow him. They are to my back so they did not see my face. You go to the motel, get a secured line and find out the latest on this case. Tell the Agency that I am following a possible member of the bird gang."

David followed the man out of the café and to a door of the shipping warehouse. This tall skinny man quickly unlocked and entered the building. He disappeared before the door completely shut allowing David to catch and hold the door open until he was inside without being noticed. The man walked down the hall and to two skids of crates with shipping labels. David hid in the shadows. *Why is there no guard on duty in this building*, David questioned to himself. The man opened up one of the cartons and took out a box probably containing one of the drug filled birds. It wasn't long before the man closed the carton and took off back down the hall to the door where he came in. David waited in the shadows until he was sure the man was out the door they both came in. Then he hurried over to the same two skids. He set two explosive charges on the sides of each crate, set

*The Garden*

the timer for 3 hours and left by another door. Then it was back to the hotel.

It was exactly three hours later that David heard a muffled explosion from the building about a block from his motel room window. About 15 minutes later he saw the building in flames.

In the morning both agents awoke at 5:30 and met in the lobby. "David," Jennifer said, "how did you make out last night? I was a little worried about you."

"Jennifer, I think that our task in this place is now complete," he responded. "I will tell you about it on our way to the airport."

They called for a cab and were about to depart and on their way to the airport. A new assignment was waiting for them.

"Why are we leaving before our work here is done?" She asked.

"All of the birds are now destroyed," David said. "I'm sure that you heard the explosion about 8 p.m. last night."

"As a matter of fact, I did and I wondered what it was," Jennifer responded. "I never saw a building burning up so fast as that one."

"Well, it was several 100,000s of dollars' worth of drugs in stuffed birds going up in smoke."

"So, what do we do now?" Jennifer asked.

"Wait for instructions from our agency, I guess."

The next thing that occurred was totally unexpected by both agents. As they were about to leave the hotel in a cab on their way to the airport, David walked around the back of the cab to open the door and assist Jennifer. When he was at the back of the cab, the trunk door suddenly opened. A dark haired black bearded man in a white sweatshirt suddenly appeared jumping out and at the same time pushing David backwards unto the ground. The man opened the door for Jennifer, pulled out a gun, and pushed her into the car. "Привод Привод," (Russian for

*The Garden*

'Drive, Drive'.) he shouted to the cab driver as he jumped into the car and slammed the door. *Jennifer has just been kidnapped and I was helpless,* David thought. He had his gun ready but it was too late.

Jennifer was taken by surprise. Two thoughts ran through her mind. Was this related to the destruction of the drug filled birds that David accomplished a few hours before? Did David notice what was going on and could he have stop my abduction? She reached for her gun—it was in her bag in the trunk. The man who forced her into the cab and entered himself had a gun on her. It appeared that the cab driver was not part of the kidnapping, but she couldn't be sure. Finally, she wondered if this action had anything to do with a sex kidnapping ring—part of the human trafficking trade going on in the world. It had been reported by the Agency that this city was a hotbed for this activity as a gathering and transporting location. David was caught off guard by this act and needed to act immediately.

"What do you want from me?" Jennifer loudly ask her abductor, not knowing the language he spoke. He remained quiet. She assumed he was Russian of which she knew none of the language. He secured Jennifer's two wrists together with black masking tape in one hand while holding his gun with the other. He then taped her mouth shut. The car drove for 2 miles and stopped in the back of a small motel by the Black Sea shore. The man motioned with his gun for her to get out of the cab. They both did and walked inside the motel, down the hall and into an unlocked room. Inside and sitting on the bed were 5 other young women. Jennifer knew immediately what was going on. Another man came out of the bathroom and motioned for Jennifer to sit on the bed alongside one of the other women. Now there were 3 women on each side of the bed—a total of 6 women probably headed for a nightmare of abuse, slavery, sex exploitation, misery, and eventual death.

All of a sudden the man standing by the bed shot the man from the bathroom, for some unknown reason. The harsh action was probably ordered by the head of the gang. It may have been

*The Garden*

done to scare the 6 girls into submitting to the orders that they were to be given later in their business transaction.

Meanwhile, David had contacted the agency over a secured line and informed them of the latest development. "What is going on with the kidnapping of Jennifer?" David asked. The person at the other end of the communication waited for a few seconds while he transferred the call to someone else.

"David," the familiar voice spoke, "what's going on?"

"Is this Max?" David asked. "That's what I want to know. Jennifer has just been kidnapped. It happened right in front of the motel we were staying at. That's getting pretty bold."

"It is, and it is how this group of sex abductors is working. Their method is to capture at least 6 young women and take them in a bus to where they are transported to the place where they are sold to the highest bidder in an auction. So what you need to look for," Max said, "is a medium size bus. I will quickly search this area for the bus. We are on it now," Max answered, "and we will let you know very shortly."

Jennifer sat on the bed in the motel wondering what would happen next. She was able to push a button on her waist activating the distress signal to satellite and then to the agency. It was then sent to David where he received it inside his motel lobby. Within 3 minutes he was informed that a small bus was parked two miles from the motel where Jennifer was held hostage. David called for a cab.

"Where to Sir?" the cab driver asked. David immediately recognized the same cab driver as the one that drove away with Jennifer. He suspected that this guy was connected with the kidnappers and David was ready for any violent action. He also wasn't sure how involved local officials may be connected with this group of thugs. Maybe this cab driver was involved as a driver of the cab pickup and/or bus driver—maybe both. David decided to take a chance.

"Bring me to the same motel." David said.

"Ok." The cab driver responded. "However, I ask that you provide me with a good tip, even though the organization pays me for my services."

"No problem, here is a U.S. 50 dollar bill," he said. As he handed the cab driver the bill, David noticed that he had a bulge on the right side of his chest, which indicated a hand gun. The only thing he could think of was to send a message to Jennifer to keep calm and to pray. As he kept his eyes on the cab driver, he prayed: *Lord we need your help again. Please send an angel to Jennifer and to me. Amen.*

The driver drove to the edge of town to the same motel where Jennifer had been taken and was being held.

"Where do you want to be let off?" he asked David.

"Take me to the office, I need to pay them some money."

Once David was let off and the cab driver had driven off, David walked to an alley and called the agency back in the U.S. The call went directly to his immediate boss. What's the latest, David?" his boss asked.

"I found where Jennifer is and I am wondering how we can secure and rescue her without her abductors hurting her. I am guessing that there may be other girls in a room with her."

"Don't do anything yet, I will get a couple of helicopters with rescue teams to sit close by and wait. See if you can find out the room number where Jennifer is in and if there are any other women in the room."

"Give me a few minutes and I will call you back," David answered. He walked into the motel lobby and down the hallway. There were only 3 cars in the parking lot which indicated that the motel was almost empty. As he walked past the doors he noticed the one at the end of the hall had a 'do not disturb' sign on the door knob. He stopped and listened for any sounds from inside the room. Suddenly a cell phone rang from inside the room.

A man answered, "I'm here, what's up?" This was followed by a brief pause. "I have 6 girls sitting and tied up on the bed. When will the bus be here?" he continued. At that point David knew for certain that the operation was a human trafficking situation. He had to think and act quickly. There was no way of

## The Garden

knowing when the bus picking them up would be at the motel. From the comments of the man, David assumed that there was only one person beside the girls inside the room. He decided to call for the rescue helicopter immediately, which he did as he waited by the door. Then David readied his gun and walked quietly up to the room door. With one kick the door flew open, breaking loose the chain lock. He immediately spotted the man sitting at the table. "Put your hands up or I will shoot you in the head!" David shouted. The man quickly threw up his hands. David walked behind him and hit the man on the head knocking him out cold. The man fell to the floor. It was then that David noticed that the other man was lying on the floor shot through the head.

The girls on the bed were overjoyed, indicated by their movement and closed mouth unison sound. They all had masking tape over their mouths. "Go to the back door of the motel where there will be 6 girls to rescue," David said in his communication to the rescue crew. "Hurry, before their transport bus gets here." David hadn't had the time yet to verily that Jennifer was among the capture girls. He turned toward the bed and saw that she was one of them.

David quickly and carefully removed the masking tape from the hands and mouths of all 6 women, starting with Jennifer. She grabbed him and gave him a hug and kiss, knowing full well that she may have been headed for a life of abuse and misery had it not been for his rescue effort. It was also an answer to prayer. As he removed the masking tape from the other women, they too gave David a quick hug. "Be as quiet as you can, girls," David said to them."

"We are landing David," a voice came over the voice box attached to his belt.

"Be sure to land near the back door," David responded.

"In 30 seconds," was the response from the rescue helicopter? David quickly used the same roll of masking tape used to secure the girls, to secure the man that he had just knocked out. His hands and feet were now taped and his mouth was sealed. The girls watched David and gave him a silent round of applause.

Soon the noise of a helicopter was heard above the motel and landed a few seconds later. The ladies were quickly ushered into the helicopter and offered some food and water. David stayed behind with Jennifer to wait for the small bus which hopefully would contain the members of the human trafficking operation.

David had his gun loaded and was ready for any violent confrontation. There were an additional four policemen from the country of the Turkey that the Agency had contacted. It was a trustworthy group of officers that had been involved with the human trafficking work with the Agency for two years. Their main task was to investigate the drug traffic and the seizure of said drugs. They were suddenly thrown into the task of dealing with human trafficking. This Turkish drug force had their eyes on this particular motel for a while and the big break had finally occurred.

David and Jennifer remained in the same room. Their instructions were to capture the thugs alive so that the Agency and the Turkish government could interrogate them and gain information that could be used in a trial against them.

It wasn't long before the bus came to transport the expected captured girls to the place where they would be auctioned off as sex slaves. "Get ready Jennifer—expect anything." The bus drove up to the back door. The driver, expecting the door to open and the girls to be led out, was puzzled when it didn't happen. One other person, one of the gang's principals stepped out first. The driver followed.

"Hold it right there!" David yelled out. "Put your hands up." Both the bus driver and the other passenger quickly pulled out their guns. Even before they had a chance to aim their weapons, David fired twice, shooting the weapons out of their hands. Keeping his gun aimed at the two thugs, they ran to them and Jennifer quickly placed handcuffs on their wrists. "Ok," David said into his communication piece, "come and get your men."

The Turkish police soon came from around the corner and had the four men—the two men that came in the bus, the man who was with the girls in the room, and the desk clerk were all led away in handcuffs.

*The Garden*

David and Jennifer went to a different hotel to stay the rest of the day and wait to receive their next assignment. They were eating lunch at about 2 pm when Jennifer said to David. "David, you never answered a question of mine."

"What question was that?" he responded.

"About settling down someday," she answered.

"So you think that you and I should hitch up together on a wagon and pull it down the road?" David answered with what he was sure she had in mind. "Do you mean get married?"

"Something like that," Jennifer answered in agreement in a slow and mumbled voice. She was surprised at his comment.

He was quiet for a moment as he was thinking of how he should answer his agent partner. He knew that she probably wouldn't like the answer, but he needed to be direct and tell her the truth.

"Well, Jennifer, it's like this. Whatever the lord wants me to do." He stopped at that point and waited for her response.

"I knew that would be your answer, David—it's a safe one." Again David waited for any further response, not wanting to commit himself. Finally he decided to not keep Jennifer hanging and gave her a definitive answer.

"Look, Jennifer. You are a fine woman. You and I have the same spiritual values and similar backgrounds. However, our lives are still ongoing and we don't know what our immediate future will hold. I believe that God permitted me to join the agency as a means of serving him. And, I suspect that He did the same for you. We do not know what the future holds, only that we know who holds the future. I advise that you concentrate on your boyfriend and pray that God will guide you in whatever decision you make."

This time Jennifer was quiet for a while. Finally, she took a deep breath and spoke. "David, you are so correct. In our current occupations, the future is not up to us. We just need to do the best we can for the security of our nation. I guess that is how we serve Him"

They stayed that night in the motel and were each on different aircraft the next morning. They hugged each other before boarding and got on their separate aircraft, neither of them knowing their exact final destination. They both had the same idea that they would probably be paired up again sometime in the future.

While on the aircraft, David received a message from the Agency headquarters in Virginia advising him on his next assignment. He was going to Saint Joseph, Missouri to investigate a trucking company that was involved with the transport of drugs from Mexico to Canada. The Agency had stumbled onto a communique that indicated that this trucking company was having various drugs picked up by one of their drivers once a month. The drugs would show up on the streets in Winnipeg a week or so later. The Agency was asked by the Canadian Drug Enforcement to intercept a shipment, get the people arrested, and destroy the smuggled goods.

David rented a car at the Saint Joseph airport and headed for a motel. When arriving at the motel he called the Agency and got his friend Max on the phone. "Max, how are you?" Max was the head of the Agency's drug smuggling division.

"David, my good friend, I am fine and hope you are the same." Max started the Agency in the early months of year 2000 and had built it along with some of the best agents in the US. "Where are you staying?"

"I am at a Super 8 motel along I-29 just on the outskirts of Saint Jo., Missouri. What have you got for me on this drug smuggling case?"

"Well, not much, David," Max stated with some disappointment in his voice. "It is a small operation with only one truck driver involved. He has connections with some of the major drug kingpins in Mexico and some of the South American countries. We do know that he knows people in St. Jo and the trucks he uses are leased from the Acme Trucking Company. The Canadian officials have told us that this particular truck shows up on the first day of the month with freight from various places in Mexico and Texas. Soon after, the drugs show up on the streets in Winnipeg and the surrounding communities. The officials in Canada have decided to have us investigate them, blow the whistle, and get the truck company and the driver arrested. We really do not know if any of the local officials in any of the countries are involved." Both David and Max paused for a moment while they were both wondering what to say next. Finally David spoke.

"Do you have a description of the truck driver?" David asked.

"He is a medium size male who usually wears a baseball cap. We suspect he stays at a local motel and carries a box or case of the drugs with him into the motel at night. We have had the truck raided there at Saint Joe but we could not find anything."

"Ok," David replied, "I will take it from there." As soon as David got off the phone, he looked up the Acme Trucking Company and the Motels close by. He found that a Motel 6 was next to the truck company. David decided to start there and see where it would lead him.

If the truck driver stayed there, chances were that he had a reservation for the night he would pull into St. Joseph. Once David had checked into the Super 8, he headed over to the Motel 6. He walked in and up to the front desk. "Can I help you sir," the clerk said in a kind voice. "Yes you can," David answered in a curious voice. "I am looking for an individual whom I met the last time I was through St. Jo. He stayed either at this Motel or the Super 8. It was on the last days of the previous month. He is a truck driver on his way to Canada, and wore a baseball cap. I met him in a Chinese restaurant across the freeway. He was looking for a good resort to stay with his family in Missouri. I

*The Garden*

got his address and phone number, but lost it. I promised I would send him some information. That is all the info I can remember and was hoping that you would have some information to help me." The desk clerk thought for a minute and then looked at his computer.

"It seems that I remember that particular individual. He comes through here once a month. I remember him because he gave me a crate of peaches on one of his trips. Let me see if I can find his name." It didn't take long until the clerk found the information. "Here it is. His name is Nosnhoj Yenoom. I believe he is foreign born and speaks with quite an accent. He speaks a South American language." David had hit the jackpot with his first inquiry.

"Thank you sir," David said to the desk clerk. "I will see if I can get a hold of him."

"By the way, he is due to check in here in 2 days," the desk clerk added. "That is when his reservation is for."

"Oh, when he does check in, please don't tell him that Jake wants to see him. I want it to be a surprise."

"Gotch ya," the desk clerk said. With that, David walked out and immediately called the Agency with the information. They would need to do an online investigation of Mr. Yenoom.

"David, this Andrew at the Agency. I was told that upon receiving some concrete information in this case to dispatch a partner to you. His name is Leo Sahlberg. I believe that you know him."

"I do indeed know him," David responded. "I know Leo very well."

"Reserve a room for him where you are staying."

Leo and David met the next morning at the St. Joe airport restaurant, had a light breakfast, and hot tea. They had met when both were teamed together in Alaska investigating a greenhouse marijuana growing farm site. They were successful in destroying the many bales of the weed and getting the principals of the drug organization arrested by the Alaskan Drug Enforcement Agency. Unfortunately, Leo was wounded by gunfire from the members of the gang running the farm. He ended up in the hospital in Anchorage with a broken leg and a grazed head. "Leo," David said, "how did you make out with your injuries?"

"I was in the hospital for two weeks," Leo responded. "Most everything has healed, although my walk is not quite what it used to be. If I do my exercises like I should, my leg will soon be back to normal, so says my doctor."

"Tell me, David, how are we going to handle this case? I've discussed it with the Agency and they say to be careful. The truck driver is a mean one."

"This guy's truck should be at the Motel tonight," David answered. He will no doubt carry the drugs into the motel room and keep them overnight. We will need to check into the same motel, in two separate ground floor rooms, keep our doors open, and the shades up. When we see a semi-truck and trailer pull up, probably in back of the motel, we will listen to what room the clerk gives him. He will go to his room and then go over to the restaurant." David waited for Leo to offer his input into the plan.

"Then we will break into his room, get the drugs, take them out to the country, and burn them in a ditch."

"Sounds good, Leo," David responded. "However, we will leave a packet of drugs on the motel table. Then we will call the local drug enforcement crew and tell them to come to the motel. The man will then get arrested. I guess they call that entrapment."

Since both agents had the entire day to spent doing almost nothing, they decided to do some sightseeing. They also took a leisurely lunch hour and discussed every subject except personal issues. They traded information and gossip about other Agency agents. They discovered that the Agency was planning on starting a retirement and savings account for their agents.

This was good news for both of them—Leo was saving money for his children's education and David still had some college loans to pay off.

Both agents took up their positions in the lobby and waited for the semi to show up that evening. It pulled in on time and pulled around to the back of the motel. Soon a medium size middle aged man entered the front door carrying two suitcases. Leo had parked himself in a soft chair on the end of the front desk, where neither the desk clerk nor the drug man could see him. David was in a chair where he could see down the hall where the drug guy was expected to enter his room.

"Hi, can I help you today?" the desk clerk asked.

"Yes, I believe you have a reservation for Thomas Canyon," he spoke to the desk clerk in an accent that was nearly impossible to understand.

"Yes, we do. Just fill this out," the clerk requested. It didn't take long and the job of checking in was complete. "Room 109. Here is your key."

"Thank you," the truck driver replied. With that the man picked up and carried the two suitcases down to Room 109. He soon emerged and walked back to the desk. "Can you wake me up at 5 am? I need to get going by 6 am.

"Yes, we can," the desk clerk responded.

"I am going over to the Chinese food place. See you later." That was a signal that David and Leo were waiting for. As soon as he was out the door, David walked to room 109 and unlocked the door. David was an expert in unlocking locked doors in motels. He had learned this trick when he was in Agency training. Soon Leo joined him in the room and together they opened the two suitcases. They took out all of the packages of drugs and placed them in plastic laundry bags, leaving one package on the room table.

They rushed out the back door to David's rental car and drove out in to the country. They found an abandoned farm with a grove of trees. It didn't take long to burn the packages of drugs. David then called the local drug enforcement Agency. "Mike, this is David. Go ahead and go to room 109 of the Motel 6 in St. Jo. The drug guy is across the street eating Chinese."

The two agents went back to the motel to serve as backup for the local drug enforcement police. The drug man returned from Chinese restaurant and didn't become aware of the situation until he saw that his motel door was open. He walked in to find 3 policeman standing in various parts of the motel room with guns drawn and pointing at the man. After disarming him he was led out of the motel and placed in a squad car to be transported to a jail cell.

David and Leo met with the police force and exchanged information, after which the two Agency agents went to the truck parked in back of the motel to see if any additional drugs were located somewhere inside. Nothing was found. The agents drove to the airport where they would catch a plane to two separate cities.

It was time for David to take another vacation. He could go to any country in the world with the Agency paying for it, but what would he do, other than lay on a beach somewhere and get a tan, or maybe get sunburned. He did have some unique seeds that he had collected from farmer's markets and gardeners in his travels in various countries. Of course, he was unsure if these seeds would grow in the northern climate.

He called Helen and asked her if there was anything that she needed for her garden. "I could use some chemical to kill the weeds that are growing around the outside fence," she responded. "Also, see if you can find some ghost pepper plants and seeds."

"I will do that,' David answered.

# Chapter 8

When David arrived in Northern Minnesota, he found Helen and his dad working in the garden. They were busy tying up the tomatoes and peppers so the weight of the fruit would not break the branches. He walked to the fence surrounding the garden and read out loud a sign that Helen and he had painted prior to his leaving for college:

May God bless this garden and multiply it greatly.

May He also keep the rabbits out.

He stood outside of the garden fence for a while just watching the busy gardeners. Finally they noticed their son.

"David!" Helen said as she excitedly dropped the ball of bailing twine. "The traveling son has arrived home." David's dad came over to give him a big hug. "All that we are missing, is Angie." David used Helen's comment to ask what was really on his mind.

"What have you heard from Angie?" David asked with hopeful anticipation. Both Helen and Ralph's facial expression suddenly turned cool. David could tell that the news was not good.

"David, we are worried about her. She in living in an area in the Twin Cities where there are some unsavory characters."

"What do you mean unsavory characters?" David asked with partial understanding of what was meant considering Angie's past and the people she associated with in high school.

*The Garden*

"She lives in an area where there is much crime, drug abuse, and prostitution. She seems to like her job, but we do not trust where she is living," Helen responded.

"So, how is the gardening going, and the veggie market? David had decided to change the subject to something more positive.

"Things are growing great!" Ralph replied. "We are looking for a good crop of almost everything." Just then a car stopped on the street and a man walked up to the garden fence.

"I am looking for David Norby," the man announced.

"I am he," David answered. "Max, how are you?" It was one of the principles from the Agency. David did not introduce Max to Helen and Ralph for security reasons.

"We need to talk, David. Let's go to my car."

"Excuse us, mom and dad," David said as he turned to them." Both men walked to Max's car and climbed in. "What's up Max?"

"The Agency has been contacted to be on the lookout for human trafficking in and around the Twin Cities area. This awareness also extends into the small towns around the twin cities."

"So how will we get involved?" David asked.

"We will let you know. Just be prepared for when we call you, and be on the lookout for this type of activity. This activity is a horrible menace to our society and many young kids are getting sucked into it without warning."

After Max had gone, David decided to work on the garden and get his hands in the soil. He had missed all phases of planting, watering, fertilizing, and of course harvesting. He was able to get involved with some of the gardening with his work in foreign countries. However, he missed seeing the entire cycle of gardening completed—from working up the soil until the harvest was in the veggie stand, ready to be sold.

He looked around to see what needed to be done. It appeared that most everything was being accomplished by Helen and Ralph. *This is good*, David thought.

*The Garden*

As he was working, David couldn't get his mind off of the human trafficking problem that he and Max had talked about. On many occasions, as he was in airports and in crowds, he would see all of the young girls on their way to various European destinations and wonder if they would be kidnapped and forced into the bondage of human trafficking. It probably wouldn't take much convincing from their abductor since many of the girls were somewhat naïve and were looking for adventurous action. David would at the same time scan the multitudes for the man in his twin image. He somehow knew that he would someday meet up with him and even thought of various ways he could connect him with his mother's murder.

David's next assignment was in the country of Japan. His agency had become involved with an industrial espionage case. Someone was stealing top secret computers from a Japanese firm manufacturing computers and selling them to 3$^{rd}$ world countries. A device had been invented which would render a computer useless 6 months after its initial use. For what reason the perpetrators were doing this was not known. It was thought that something inside the computers was at work stealing data from accounts stored from companies.

He was headed for Washington to meet with the people who could address this particular case. He reached the airport and was met by another agent. At least he thought she was an agent.

"Mr. Norby? Mr. David Norby," she said as she recognized him from a photo she had in her pocket.

*This agent had a foreign accent in her voice,* David said to himself.

"I am that person for which you inquire. Good to meet you."

"Good to meet you too, and my name is Leah Jones." David knew from her response that this woman was Jewish and that her last name was probably fictional—her first name most likely correct. "Are you ready to go to work?"

*The Garden*

"I am ready," David said with a big smile. They walked to the front of the airport where they were to meet a special car that the agency sent and take them to the office to be versed on the new assignment. There were a total of 5 agents assigned to this case. David and Leah were to work together as a team and the other 2 males and one female were to work alone.

The case involved a small firm with a group of engineers and technicians who worked to modify at least 5 laptop computers per day and resell them to third world country buyers. Elements were being added to the computers which would obtain internal data from the company who received them, and send it back to the home office for processing. From the information obtained, the home office could steal money, securities, assets, and bonds. Once this was done, the laptop would destroy itself.

After an afternoon meeting in the Washington office of the Agency, David and Leah flew to Tokyo and arrived the next morning. The two agents took a car that was waiting for them by the airport to a small house in the residential section of Tokyo. The driver turned around and spoke. "Here is where the agency wants you to stay, at least for now." He removed their luggage from the trunk and carried both bags to the front door. David assumed that the driver worked for the agency and therefore a tip was not necessary. But Leah gave the driver an American 20 dollar bill.

They were served an American meal of steak, salad, desert, and wine in the kitchen. David settled for a diet coke from the apartment fridge. Leah took note of David omission of the wine.

"I take it that you are a teetotaler," she commented, "for some reason." She felt bad right away that she noted the exclusion. She knew from other agents that David was known for his 'straight laced' stance on a number of issues and practices. David thought a bit and replied.

"No Leah, I drink all coffees, as long as I can get my color back." Now Leah felt really bad.

"I'm sorry for my comment. I apologize."

"I accept your apology," he responded, "as long as you go with me to a place where they have some good Jewish cooking."

*The Garden*

"I know where just such a place is, only a few miles from here. You are familiar with Jewish cooking and food?"

"My best friend is a Jew, Leah," he replied.

"You'll need to tell me about him sometime," she replied, without knowing what his answer would be.

The next morning they were picked up by the same driver and brought to the Japan Agency office where the 5 agents were gathered. Some of the agents were somewhat acquainted with each other. After some small talk within the group, the office head brought the gathering to order. "First of all we need to bring all of you up-to-date with this particular case. We have done research and investigation on this company in a manner such that they have no idea that they are suspected of wrongdoing. Their plant is in the basement of a building about a mile from here. Somehow we need to infiltrate the group and find a way to destroy their computer modification techniques and obtain evidence so that we can have them arrested. These are American built computers they are using and as such, there is no law broken in Japan. It's only when they start stealing securities and funds from other firms in the United States that the law is broken and it's a federal crime." David raised his hand and asked a question.

"Will we be breaking any U.S. laws if we can destroy the computer they are working on?" The Agency head thought for a moment and answered.

"Not that I am aware of." So, you will each receive a folder which will tell what your particular assignment will be in this case."

David and Leah took their folders from a secretary and went to a private room to read and study the information contained in the folder. "This is not going to be easy, David." she said. "Maybe the first thing we should do is to visit the building where they are working," Leah commented. "Maybe one of us should apply for work there."

*The Garden*

"Good idea Leah," David responded. "Let's flip a coin to see who will apply."

"Then what will the loser or winner do?" Leah asked.

"Maybe peruse the building to see how we could gain an entrance," David responded. Leah took out a quarter and flipped it. While it was in the air, she called out.

"Heads!" The coin landed on the table, heads. "I win and I will apply for a job. You, partner, will examine the building and find a way to break into it."

Leah wrote down on a piece of paper the target company's address and left the folder with the Agency secretary. David walked part way to the building with her and then said goodbye. He walked in, found the elevator, and punched the basement floor elevator button. Immediately, a rectangular light came on. It was a warning message in Japanese and English. "The floor you have pressed is a secure floor. Please see the building main desk."

David then punched the up button of the elevator and entered. When he walked off he was on the roof. Right away he was familiar with what he saw—a group of rooftop gardens. There were some people working on some short raised bed gardens. David knew that the beds could not be too high because of the weight exerted on the roof. One of the people who looked like she may be from the U. S. asked David. "Can I help you?" One of David's question was answered—she spoke perfect English.

"Yes," he answered. "I am looking for a spot on a rooftop to grow a garden." The woman stopped what she was doing and looked at David.

"You should go down to the first floor and see the people in room 109. They will help you." She was obviously an American from the way she spoke.

"Thank you, I will do that." On the first floor David found room 109. The lady was Japanese. "How can I get a space on the roof to grow a garden?"

"Here is a form for you to fill out. Just take the elevator to the top floor and make a diagram of where you wish to place your rooftop garden. Bring the completed form and diagram back here and we will look it over and approve, if it looks good."

David took the same elevator to the 15th floor and began to walk around. He needed to find a place where the sun would give maximum exposure to the raised bed. More important, he needed to use the rooftop location to somehow spy on the computer company in the basement. *How could I do that*, he asked himself. The answer to that question was with the use of sophisticated instruments. He knew that the computer operation was on the southeast corner of the building and that is the location that would provide good sun exposure. He drew a diagram, sat down in a chair and completed the application.

Leah was successful in applying and securing an assembly and testing job with the computer company. She and David met that evening at a small café and began to coordinate a plan to infiltrate the computer company. "The first thing we need to do is to propose our plan to the Agency tomorrow morning at our meeting," David suggested. "I will lower a wire down from the roof with our most sophisticated tiny microphone attached. It will pick up sounds within the room, send them through a device that will separate many different sounds and conversations, then amplify them, filter, and block out interference. So Leah, what kind of a job will you be doing?"

"I will be working in the shipping and receiving department," she answered, "to start with."

"Good," David responded with a positive tone, "you will probably be moved around as a utility person. The Agency informed me this morning that the company moves people around so they will not get to be too much of an expert in any one job. They may gain too much access to too much information."

*The Garden*

   David was successful in installing the microphone wire from the top of the building. He then attached the mike on to the window outside of the company's assembly area. The color of the wire was the same as the building so it would not be easily noticed. He then went back on the roof and connected the top of the wire to a transmitter.
   Leah was friendly to everyone she worked with, recorded their names and positions, along with various pertinent information. This was done in her memory. She would then place it on her laptop computer at night in her apartment. She and David would meet in one of their apartments each night to discuss the day's activities. David was finding that some of the people growing veggies and flowers on the roof were also working for the computer company. On a Tuesday night the two of them met at a restaurant that served kosher food. He had the same food that Leah ordered. "I take it you have eaten here before, Leah," he said.
   "Yes, I have been here a few times. The food is good and the head chef is Jewish direct from Israel. All of the other kitchen help are Japanese. They all are respectful to our culture even keeping the dairy and meat in separate refrigerators."
   "OK, we need to discuss our next move on the company," David interrupted the Kosher talk. "The Agency has caught wind of a plan to move their entire operation to another country. What they want us to do is to destroy all of the finished units prior to their shipping the Friday a week from now. The Agency now has a list of all of the principals of the company and will arrest them before the move."
   "We will need to break in somehow and arm the computers with small explosives," Leah added. "That is my expertise—explosives."
   "I will work on breaking into the shipping room," David responded. The remainder of the dinner meeting was spent on small talk. David sensed that Leah wanted to ask him a question.
   "David," she began, "you mentioned something when we first met that I have been wondering about. You said that you had

*The Garden*

a person who was your best friend. You said 'my best friend is Jewish.' Is that person a male or female?"

David smiled and then answered, "I do remember when I said that. My best friend is a male. He has been my friend since I was 8 years old. I give him the credit for getting me out of multiple life threatening difficulties. I talk to him every day."

"Where does he live?" Leah asked with slight skeptic look. David wondered how long he could keep her strung along.

"He was in Jerusalem at various times," David responded.

"Was he born in Israel?" Leah asked.

"Actually, Leah, He was born in a town south of Jerusalem called Bethlehem." Leah was quiet for a number of seconds, as she finally caught on and where this discussion was going.

"Let's talk shop, David," she said indicating that she wished to change the subject. "What is our next move?"

"Tomorrow morning I will break into the assembly area and place some explosives that you will provide me with, on each computer. The Agency will notify the Tokyo drug enforcement division and they will arrest all of the people in that office as they come to work."

The next morning David broke into the computer company at 4 a.m. and armed each of 25 in-process computers with an explosive device set to go off at 6:45, 15 minutes prior to starting time.

The 25 explosions went off almost at the same time, causing the entire first 3 floors to shake as though a small earthquake had taken place. Fortunately, the building did not catch fire and no one was hurt.

The plan worked perfectly with all of the computers being destroyed, everyone in the company arrested, and information stored on the company's computer leading to drug arrests in 6 different countries.

David and Leah met two members of the Agency at the airport in a private meeting room. "The Agency congratulates both

## The Garden

of you on a job well done. The computers have been destroyed and the Japanese Government has arrested all of the principals. They will be sent back to their home countries and may even face charges there."

"Thank you," Leah responded. "I am ready for a vacation."

"Both of you are and here are your tickets for home," the Agency head stated. "Best wishes to both of you."

The next morning they both went to the airport only to find out that their flight had been cancelled because of a typhoon in the Pacific. "Now what do we do," Leah asked.

"I don't know about you," David answered, "but I am going back to that building to help that woman garden on the roof top. If you want, I will call the Agency and have them reserve two rooms at the same motel for us. And remember, you owe me another trip to a Jewish Deli."

By 1 PM the two agents were on top of the same building where there were a number of raised beds were located. David saw the same woman that he had spoken to when he inquired about having a rooftop raised bed. "Hi, I see you are still working at trying to grow some plants."

"Yes, I am," she spoke in a disappointed tone. David could see that she had a doubtful expression as if she didn't know what she was doing.

"Can I be of any help to you," he asked?

"Yes you can," she responded. "What do you know about growing a garden in a raised bed?"

"On a rooftop?" David added to her question.

"Exactly," she spoke with a little added happiness in her voice.

"Well," he replied, "do you have any plants or seeds? I see that you have plenty of black dirt on the bed. It looks very rich." She emptied a paper bag on a small table. Then she sat down on another raised bed. "Let's start with the carrots." They planted two rows of the carrots in two rows across from side to side. Then it was on to the mustard green and beets. By the time

*The Garden*

an hour had gone, they had the entire bed planted. Leah just watched the entire planting activity without saying a word. The woman was very impressed and seemed happy.

"Thank you for your help. I will remember you when I harvest the crop in a few months."

It was time to eat and Leah spoke up. "Ok David, let's go have some Kosher food. I will buy."

"Sounds great, I'm hungry." They took a taxi to a Japanese restaurant about 3 miles from the motel. The hostess showed them to a padded booth in the back of the deli. After receiving the menus and the water they ordered from the waitress, they studied the menu as to what they wanted to eat. Leah ordered first.

"This place also serves kosher food. I will take a grilled Ruben, a cup of matzo ball soup, and a potato Knish. You're next David."

"I tell you what," David responded, "Give me a bowl of matzo ball soup, a potato knish, and I will help Leah eat her Ruben. I see the sandwich that guy over there is eating and I don't think Leah can eat all of hers."

"You are so right David, thank you."

# Chapter 9

It was time for another break from work. David tried to do something to relax himself from the stressful months with Agency. The tasks were often traumatic, at times life threatening, and again he didn't know how much more he could take of it. He kept in his tiny "green book" a list of career occupations he would rather do someday. The reason it was called a green book was because the list represented potential greener pastures. David would often read the list to himself to get his mind back to being hopeful. He also knew that for some strange reason, God had placed him in this line of work. Other items in the book were of a personal nature. It was tiny, 2 inches by 3 inches, and was kept inside his large belt buckle.

On his way back to his home in Northern Minnesota, he stopped in Minneapolis to see his childhood friend, Angie. She had completed her sentence at a rehab center for involvement in drugs and was attempting to go straight by working in a food processing factory during the day and cleaning apartments at night. The Agency checked on her progress at the request of David. They would prefer to do that rather than having him contact her. She was working on the floor of the factory when David arrived at the address where the factory was located. He waited in the factory lobby. Soon this beautiful girl appeared in the doorway of the lobby waiting area. "Angie," David yelled out. "How are you?" She had matured into a beautiful and attractive woman since the last time he had seen her.

"I am fine," she answered. "How are you?"

"A little tired, but healthy," he answered. "I am on my way to our home to help your mom and my dad in the garden. I was hoping that you could come with me."

"I would like to, but I have spent my vacation time already," Angie answered disappointedly. "I would like to spend time at home for a weekend, but it would be too short a time to drive that distance. Besides, I still don't have a car. They took my driver's license away when I got too many D.U.I.s. How about if you spend a couple days here. You can stay in my apartment and sleep on the couch."

"Maybe I will spend the night," he answered.

"Can you give me a ride home from work?" Angie asked. "Since I don't have a car I need to take a bus every day. You can wait in the office waiting room for the next 4 hours."

"I will gladly do that," he answered. "I have some paperwork to catch up on." David sat for the next 3 hours thinking about Angie and engaged in prayer about many areas of his and her life. His life as an agent had been successful, but filled with near death situations, temptations from a variety of very beautiful women, etc. He had maintained his boyhood desire of someday marrying Angie. Maybe this was only a boyhood fantasy dream that needed to be disregarded with the passage of time and because of the effects of a bad life Angie had experienced since childhood. David knew what her personal life had been like. On the other hand, his thought process had maintained this dream of marriage for some reason. David knew it was God that kept bringing her back to this thought process. What God's purpose was to permit this was always a question on his mind? David knew that in time it would be revealed.

"Mr. Norby," a voice interrupted his thinking, "Angie asked me to bring you this coffee and cookies from the break room. She said that she didn't want you to get thirsty or hungry. Are you her boyfriend?" The woman was an office secretary.

*The Garden*

"Whatever she has told you," he uttered. "She and I were neighbors, went to the same school in the same grade, graduated together and have maintained a long distance communication relationship over the months and years. I am a boy and I am her friend—yes."

"Sounds like you two are more than just acquaintances," the woman commented.

"So how has Angie been doing?" David questioned the woman. The middle aged woman sat down on the office sofa besides him, took a deep breath and began to talk about Angie.

"She seems both happy and unhappy. She spent time in a rehab/jail facility, as you probably know. She came to work here and has done an excellent job for the company. As far as I can see, she has maintained her drug free life style. Many of our single and even married guys have asked her out, but she refuses. She told me that these guys would only tempt her with booze and drugs and she knows that she probably couldn't resist the temptation. She said to me 'they are only after one thing.' It seems like some force is keeping her anchored." David knew what, or rather, Who that was. The woman stood up and started to walk back to her desk. She turned around quickly and added, "she has been seeing an unsavory character that some of us girls are worried about."

"What kind of a person is this guy and what is it that makes you worry about Angie?" David asked.

"He is trying to talk her into moving out of the country." That statement told David volumes about this particular individual's character.

"Thank you ma'am," he said as she walked away. He placed his head on the sofa back and closed his eyes. He began to think about the past many months and his difficult and near death experiences. He also thought about the character who was trying to talk Abby into going to Europe. It sounded like a human trafficking scenario. One thought led to another and he was soon sleeping. That was when he begin to dream. He was in a strange country with Angie and she turned up missing. The Agency attempted to find her but with no leads or trail to follow.

## The Garden

The next part of the dream involved the images of the man that killed David's mother. The first image was first seen by David when he witnessed the actual murder—the second of the same man in an airport. That is when the dream ended.

"David, wake up!" Angie said, as she touched his hair, "It is time to leave."

"OK, I'm ready," he responded. "I guess I must have dozed off." He suddenly had a strange feeling that he needed to prepare himself for such a dream actually happening. He knew what to do.

They drove to Angie's apartment. It was on the south side of downtown Minneapolis. Angie was tired and she set her head on a pillow David placed for her on the back of the front seat. He was quiet while she dozed off. *We will talk later,"* David thought to himself. They were soon at a house where the G.P.S. directed. "Is this where your apartment is, Angie?"

"Exactly," she answered. "Grab your suitcase and follow me."

"You live in the jungle area of town, where the pots and pans salesmen hang out. Is that true?"

"It is true," Angie answered. "Salesman are always trying to sell the single girls housewares." They walked in the front door and into one of four apartments in the building. Each apartment had an upstairs and a basement. "You can sleep in the upstairs bedroom," Angie told David.

"Thank you. Let me take you out for supper," David said.

"That would be great David, I don't feel like cooking tonight. There is a good place to eat downtown. They just opened about a year ago." After Angie washed up and changed clothes, they both got into David's car again and drove a few blocks to an old storefront building that had been converted into a small restaurant. They found a booth and were soon drinking water that the waitress brought them. They sat quietly for about 30 seconds both wondering what they should talk about. David decided to begin.

"Angie, what is new with you?" He sensed that she had many personal items which she wanted to share. There was her drug addiction, the time spent in rehab facility, her mother Helen, and Helen's marriage to David's father. Angie continued the discussion.

"David, you have been in dangerous situations many times in your work, haven't you? I know that I shouldn't be asking about this subject, but I keep worrying about it."

"Yes I have," he answered. "All I can say is that I need constant prayer. Now, I would like to do something for you."

"What's on your mind, David?'

"To tell the truth, I am worried about you being here in a big city. There are reports of young girls being kidnapped and taken to faraway locations for various evil reasons."

"Really." Angie replied, in a manner that told David that she was probably not fully aware of such happenings.

"Yes, really Angie. So, I want you to wear a tiny computer chip. This chip will tell me where you are at all times. I have my Agency's permission to have you wear it."

"So where do I wear the chip?" she asked.

"I want you to wear it as an earring or a decorative button on your blouse or coat. Can you do that?" David waited for a few seconds while Angie pondered about what David had just proposed to her.

"That would be fine, David," she answered.

The two friends completed their meal and headed back to Angie's apartment. When they returned, David grabbed a small box from his suitcase. "This contains a tiny chip inside an earring. David attached the earring to her earlobe. He immediately called the Agency. "Is Max there," he asked. There was a short pause while the Agency located Max.

"David, what can I do for you?"

"Max, I have another person using the chip. Can you see if it's going through?"

"It is," Max replied. "Is this your friend you were talking about the last time you were here?"

"It is."

The two childhood friends talked until 11 pm about many subjects. David kept clear of discussing anything having to do with the bible, God, Christianity, church involvement, and related topics. It was somewhat difficult for David to do this since he knew that it was these topics that Angie needed to hear. He knew that he was probably the only bible that Angie ever read. He just needed to be her friend.

The next morning David continued on his travel to Dalestown. It was great to once again return to working with the soil. Helen was glad that David was able to plant, fertilize, harvest, or sell garden plants at least once every year. The garden was now 4 times as large as when David left for college. His father and Helen were happy in their marriage and involved with church, the community, and working sometimes 10 to 14 hours in a day in the garden. Even though David and Helen had begun the garden enterprise, the proceeds now belonged entirely to his father and Helen.

He looked around to see where he could make improvements in the garden and the vegetable stand. Helen had made a weekly list of several items to be worked on. David spent the next 5 days working on this list. The work was both relaxing and fun.

On his way back to the airport, David received a coded message from the Agency. He looked at it and became startled. It was about Angie. She was missing from work for the second day. For some reason the Agency had become involved. David wondered why. Within another 2 minutes another message came through. '*Your friend has been kidnapped by a foreign gang and is believed to be headed for a foreign country. Stay tuned for a reassignment.*' This situation was important enough for the Agency to get David directly involved. He knew that the name 'foreign gang' mentioned by the Agency in the message was a code word for human trafficking. Since he had experience with this Agency matter, it was natural that he get involved. He couldn't believe

*The Garden*

that this could happen just days after he had placed a computer chip with Angie.

David immediately knew what to do. He bowed his head and began to pray silently. *Lord, I need your help once more. First of all keep Angie safe from the evil hands of her abductors. Be with the Agency and myself as we track this case. Give us wisdom to seek out where the evil thugs have taken her. Bind the hands of the enemy. Amen.*

A helicopter was waiting at the airport car rental return to take him to the Agency headquarters. He went into a conference immediately. "What do we know about Angie?" he asked the gathered group of agents. "I was notified with very little information." The head of the Agency stood up, cleared his throat, opened up a folder, and began to speak.

"We intercepted a communique yesterday afternoon from somewhere in Europe stating that there was a group of women to be auctioned off. The communique also stated the first names of the women. Angie's name was among them. We also were notified yesterday morning by the FBI that Angie was abducted from her company's parking lot as she got out of her car. At least two people saw it happen." David sat in silence for a short time. Everyone was aware that Angie was a close friend of David and were wondering how he would react. Finally, David spoke.

"I am very sorry this happened and wish to be involved with this case. I will tell you that she has two of our chips on her. One in her earring and one in her ankle bracelet." The leader stood up again and concluded the meeting by saying. "I want Jennifer and David to go right away to Angie's apartment and see if anyone had visited her. I cannot believe that she was targeted at random."

About an hour later David and Jennifer walked into Angie's apartment looking for anything that would give them a clue as to who her abductors were or where she had been taken. What they found was a phone message that Angie apparently had not listened to. The caller said that he was a life insurance salesman and wanted to meet with her. He said he would contact her at her workplace in the morning with a packet of information and a ticket to a restaurant where the insurance plan would be explained, along with a free meal. David smelled a rat immediately. He grabbed the message machine and he and Jennifer headed to the Agency office. "We need to have this message analyzed for any clues," David said.

A break in the case came when another communique was intercepted and analyzed by the agency. It seems that the location of the captured women was going to be in the country of the Ivory Coast in a jungle area. David and Jennifer were immediately on a plane for that part of the world. "Well," Jennifer began the conversation on the plane after they were settled, "we were lucky on the girls when I was captured. Whether or not we have the same good luck on this one remains to be seen."

"I believe that God will protect Angie," David commented. "He has a plan for her and for the work that she will do some day. I have prayed for her almost every day for the past few years." Jennifer knew from this comment that her desire for being with David someday was not possible. He was attached to Angie more than she thought.

When David and Jennifer landed in the country of the Ivory Coast, they went first to the police station to see if any information was available on the human trafficking activity in that country or surrounding countries. David had a stash of American money and was able to bribe one of the officials who had been working on the case. "So you're telling me that the girls are being held in a trailer inside a big garage in a jungle area until they are sold?" David confirmed what the official had told him. He then handed the official a few US $50 bills.

## The Garden

"Yes, but I don't know exactly where the trailer is located," was the official's answer. David suspected that he was still withholding important information. Using additional bribe money, David was able to extract another piece of critical information. "The jungle where the girls are being held is near the small town of Ksirf Trebla about 20 miles north of here," the official told David.

It didn't take long for the two agents to rent a small car and drive the dusty rough roads to the tiny Ivory Coast town. David made contact with his supervisor as they stopped for a necessary moment for Jennifer. "David," his super said, "what's up with your investigation? Are you making any progress?"

"We are on our way to a small town 20 miles north of where we landed—to the town of Ksirf Trebla. The information I gathered says that the kidnapped women are hidden in a trailer in the jungle north of that town. The trailer is supposedly inside a garage. My source did not say exactly where the garage is. However, Angie has a chip on her and maybe you can locate her with the use of satellite observation."

"We will see what we can do, David. But be very careful. They will shoot the girls if they find out you are about to get to them. If you are there they will shoot you first."

"How soon can you get me the location?" David asked his super.

"I just got it. You are very close. I would suggest that you drive a few more miles, hide your car, and walk the rest of the way."

"OK, thanks," David responded. They drove for another 3 miles and saw an old road going into a forest. They drove the car into the thicket and stopped. They sat in quiet for a short time. Both Jennifer and David suddenly became in deep thought. She wondered how they were going to get into the trailer without revealing themselves. Jennifer had some bad memories of when she was in the same situation that Angie was now in. She also wondered if David's judgment would be compromised being Angie was among the captured girls.

"Let's rest for a bit," she suggested.

"Sounds like a winner, Jennifer." David's thoughts were also weighing various options on how they were going to attack this situation. He had a personal interest in this case and had to be extra careful.

Since it was close to sundown, they decided to spend the night in the front seat of the car in a reclining position. Just before they finally fell asleep, Jennifer reached over and touched David's hand. He took that hand and squeezed it thinking that she may be a little frightened. After all, they were in a very dark jungle, they were alone, and wild creatures were lurking in their gloomy location.

He thought of the garden that Angie's mother, Helen, and he had started in their back yards. That thought led to his memory of his mother having been tortured and killed by some homeless thug passing through their town, and being tied up as he was forced to watch. He was now dreaming about the entire ordeal. Something clicked in his mind and for the first time he recalled all of the details. The man raped and did some very evil things to his mom and made him watch as he finally shot her. The investigating authorities could not figure out why the thug did not shoot David. For David it was not difficult for him to understand—did God have a purpose for allowing this horrible act to take place and he being a witness to the entire murder.

Both of the agents were awake at about 4 a.m. David called the Agency to get the latest on the girl hostages in the trailer. "Hey David, do you know you are only about 3 miles from where the girl's trailer is parked. We are getting information that a helicopter may be on its way to transport them to a new location, probably where they will be auctioned off to the highest bidders. You had better hurry. You have less than 2 hours." David thought for a few seconds. This was going to be a difficult rescue and nothing could go wrong.

*The Garden*

"Send me an image of the location of the trailer," David responded. "Meanwhile, we will start walking toward where we can stage the rescue."

"Exactly what do you plan to do?" The voice at the Agency asked.

"At this point I really don't know. We will have our guns ready and loaded. We need to move fast," David replied, "we'll call back when we get close to the trailer." The two agents began to walk toward where they thought the trailer would be. As they were walking he began to wonder why the coordinators of this human trafficking operation were using a trailer to store their captors. Maybe it was a fly-by-night operation. In that case they probably would be using a small guard detail in holding them. Also, what about food and toilet facilities? Was there any at all? Had any of the girls been tampered with? Were any of them injured?

"Hey David," Jennifer asked, "How much further do you think?"

"I suspect that the trailer is in that garage in that grove of trees just ahead of us. Let's rest behind these large rocks and see if we can notice any activity." They found a comfortable spot and both reclined against a big rock. All of a sudden, a door on the trailer slammed and made enough noise to alert both agents to the urgency of the moment.

"David! Did you hear that noise?" Jennifer quietly and excitedly asked.

"I heard the same thing," he responded, "At least we know that someone is, or was inside that trailer. He's walking toward a car that is under that large tree. David stopped abruptly as he peered through his binoculars.

"What's wrong David?" Jennifer asked noticing his change of pace.

"It's him," he answered with excitement.

"Who?" she asked.

"It's the man who killed my mom when I was 4. Let's go get him." They quickly moved toward the area and soon were close to the car. The man was talking on a phone. David crept close to where he was able to listen.

"We need to sell these girls quickly," the man said on the phone. "One of them is sick and one has an injured leg. I think it may be broken." At that point the man waited for the response at the other end of the call. (A 30 second pause) "Ok, I will drive and pick up the buyers and bring them back to bid on the women. What should I do with the one with the broken leg?" (Another pause) "Where should I dump the body? (Another pause) OK." David wondered if Angie was the woman with the broken leg. Whomever she was would need to have special care and it may require a slower time of rescue.

# Chapter 10

"Let's go Jennifer. We need to get the girls out of the trailer as quickly as we can," David whispered. The two agents walked as fast and quietly as they could toward the trailer. When they reached the site, they saw that the trailer door was locked. Soon the man got into a car.

David quickly opened the door of the car, grabbed the man's arm, and jerked him out of the car with enough force as to dislocate the man's arm. Realizing his own anger, David quickly prayed: *Lord, keep me from shooting this evil soul through the head. He killed my mom and needs to be punished by the law."*

The man managed to get his hand on his gun. Before he could even lift the gun to where he would have a clean shot at David, David shot at his gun and the bullet pierced his leg. David then knocked him out.

David quickly broke the lock on the trailer door and perused the inside of the dark trailer with his small flashlight. Angie was crying. "Angie, are you OK?" David yelled out.

"My leg is broken," Angie cried out in a desperate voice. "They are going to take us to some evil and sick men."

"OK girls," David shouted loud and clear, "we need to get you out of here immediately. We will free your arms and legs. Then help each other to get on your feet." David and Jennifer helped to lift each girl off the back of the truck and down to the ground. David then lifted Angie and carried her in his arms. She placed her arms around his neck still weeping and shaking from fear. "Listen up girls, we need to hide out somewhere in the forest until a rescue helicopter comes to get us."

"I will stay here and clean up," Jennifer whispered to David. What her intentions were, was to set some explosives on the truck.

"Jennifer," David said, "one other thing, use some duct tape and bind the hands and ankles of the man by the car. He is the man that killed my mother when I was a little boy. Also, tell the Agency to arrest him for the murder. Tell the Agency that the crime occurred in the state of Missouri. He also needs medical help. I shot him in the leg and I think I dislocated his shoulder."

"Will do," Jennifer responded.

"Let's go girls," David called out, "walk as fast as you can. Stay close behind me. Angie, when we walk another mile I will wrap your leg as best I can. I bet it hurts you, doesn't it."

"Yes it does," she answered trying not to cry anymore. "Maybe you could place your arm under my ankle."

Jennifer walked back to the trailer and placed 4 explosive charges in various places set to go off in 20 minutes. Then she caught up to the girls and David. They walked for another mile, found a thick brush and crawled within it. While they were walking, David called the rescue helicopter and told them to come as quickly as possible. "Ok girls, find a comfortable spot to sit or to lie down. We will soon be rescued." As they sat down, there was a series of 4 explosions at the trailer site. It was being blown up. "Bingo," David loudly announced. All of the girls applauded.

As they were laying on the forest floor, Angie laid her head on David's lap. She had a slight fever, as he could determine. He found two straight branches, took some thin rope from within his backpack, and began to splint her broken leg. "Be prepared Angie, it may hurt when I wrap this rope around the two branches. I need to do this—it may be a while before you get medical help."

"I'll try to keep from letting the pain get to me. I am so glad that you found us," she said to David.

"It really is a good thing, Angie. I think that man was planning to shoot you when they come to pick you up from the trailer. A woman with a broken leg would be of no value to them. You would have no immediate sale value to those sick men." At that point Angie grabbed David and kissed him and groaned with pain while doing it. "Be careful, Angie, so you don't further injure your leg. Do you have any idea who these other girls are? I assume they are from various countries. Did the bums hurt any of the other girls?"

"I think they raped most of them on the plane ride over to where you found us. When they took me from my company's parking lot, one of men got really mad for some reason and hit my leg. I don't think he knew that my leg was busted. I prayed to God to have them keep their mangy hands off me. One of them just carried me to the car and on to the plane. I think he was going to rape me, but I screamed with pain when he tried to pull off my clothes. We have had nothing to eat and no water."

A rescue helicopter soon reached the site where the girls and agents were hiding. They were given water, food, and medical treatment. Angie's leg was badly broken in two places. The medic tending her injury told David that some tool apparently was used to break it. She would need some delicate surgery to fully repair it.

The girls were all from the United States. The investigating officer on the helicopter was told by the girls that a private jet plane was used to pick them up and flown to the Ivory Coast.

The helicopter headed to a military hospital where they were all given a complete medical exam. Angie went into surgery for 4 hours. She was given medicine and told to stay off her feet for the next 6 weeks. A separate helicopter was dispatched to where the transport vehicle was to pick up the girl hostages. The

*The Garden*

authorities were waiting to arrest the people in the transport vehicle when it arrived. All were arrested and brought to the United States where they were formally charged.

Both Angie and David were soon back in Dalestown, Minnesota. It would take at least 6 more weeks for Angie's leg to heal so she could walk on it. David was on extended leave while he was deciding on his future. He had spent 7 years with the agency and was contemplating if he should continue. While he was waiting, some of his former partners came to visit him and obtain information and his advice. David reviewed his little green book that he kept under his big belt buckle. In this book he kept a list of the various options that he may wish to pursue after retirement.

Angie spent most of her waking time resting and reading. Angie's mother aided her as she maneuvered with the broken leg around the house and out on the lawn. The weather was warm with a soft breeze whistling through the growing garden plants and flowers. On one particular Tuesday afternoon David picked a bouquet of mixed flowers and presented them to Angie as she was asleep on a chair on the lawn. When she woke up she looked at the flowers in her lap for a few seconds. She looked at her mother. "Mom, thanks for the bouquet of flowers. They smell wonderful."

"Sorry Angie, they are not my doing." She turned toward the other end of the garden where David's dad was working.

"Ralph," she shouted, "did you pick the flowers?"

"Not me either." Ralph shouted back. Angie knew that there was only one person left to ask. Unbelievably, Angie had gone through her entire life without ever receiving a bouquet of flowers, other than one time from David when they were in high school.

"OK, David," Angie yelled out to the area of the garden where he was watering plants, "come over here." David heard Angie and accepted the invitation. He walked to where she was sitting—noticing that Ralph and Helen were winking at each other.

"David, are these flowers your doing?"

"I'm guilty, your majesty," he confessed. "They are just for you."

"Well, you have given me a big bag of jelly beans, a bible, and rescued me from the hooks of evil men. What else and what's next?" David sat down on a chair in front of Angie.

"We have had a picnic together—which you prepared, I might add. You also let me buy you dinner in Minneapolis. Our lives have intersected several times."

Over the next 6 weeks Angie's leg seemed to be get better. It was a very bad break but was healing well. She passed the day sitting in a chair watching David and her mother working in the garden. There was much time to think about her past. At one point one afternoon she asked God to cause her to fall in love with David. She knew what it was that kept her from this happening, but she was unwilling to do anything about it.

David had loved Angie since childhood and Angie was always aware of this fact. She, however was not interested in David as a teen. As time went on, she increasingly saw that he was what every woman wanted in a life's partner. She also realized that David had met some very educated women in the agency. They were very beautiful and more attractive than her. *What will David do when it comes to settling down?* She wondered, *Will he marry someone from the agency? Could I fall in love with David now that he was ready to settle down? Does David still love me and should I marry him if the opportunity presents itself?* She had a few weeks for this romantic thought process to run its course and make a decision.

"David," she asked as they were sitting in the sun room one afternoon, "Where will you live when you decide to settle down?"

*The Garden*

"Angie," he said as he began his response, "that is a very good question. I guess that is what I want to do during my time off here—decide my future." Angie sensed by his answer, that David did not have any particular romantic interest that was coupled with whatever future life he would chose. "I am open to God's calling for what He may have for me." She was quiet for a half a minute. There was one other thing that she thought of. She knew from knowing him since their youth that two people needed to be equally yoked spiritually to be happily married. Angie knew she needed to commit her life to God, but she was still not willing to do this. The bitterness and deep seated hatred she had for her father was in her way of taking that step.

"David, can I be honest and tell you how I feel and what has happened to me in the past few months and years?" David sort of knew what was coming next, but not completely. His career with the agency had kept him somewhat out of touch with Angie along with her mother and his father.

"Please do, I have lots of time."

"To start with," Angie said, "I need to say that I am sorry for all the grief that I caused you in high school. I really don't know why I did it. I think that I was jealous that you had a father and mine was missing."

"But you have one now," David responded.

"I know it, but that's now. I needed a father when I was in my formative years. I never knew him or even remember what he looked like, except for the photos that mom has. I got into trouble the last year in high school with the drugs, as you are aware of. I was using them and my source tried to get me to peddle them. Something kept me from doing that. When they approached me on that subject, a wall came up and stopped me."

"I know what that wall was, Angie," David said in an assured tone.

"What was it?" she asked.

"It was your mother's and my prayers for you."

"I suspected that is what it was, thank you."

"Angie, I am expecting a friend of mine to be here in a few minutes. Maybe we can continue this talk after dinner tonight."

## The Garden

"Sounds good," Angie answered. Just then the front doorbell rang. "I will get it." Angie answered the front door. There, dressed in clothes that did not quite fit the beautiful female standing on the porch, was an agency employee—an agent. Angie was sure of it.

"I am looking for David Norby. Do I have the right house?"

"You do," David answered. "Come right in Jennifer." Angie immediately recognized the woman who, along with David had rescued her and the other captives only a few weeks previously.

"Have a seat on the couch," Angie said.

"Thank you," Jennifer responded.

"No, thank you for your help in rescuing me," Angie said. "Would you like some coffee or tea?"

"Coffee would be fine," she responded. David wasn't quite sure exactly what Jennifer wanted from him. Maybe it was unfinished agency business, or maybe she wanted to try to convince David to keep working for the agency. Then again, maybe Jennifer had an itch for David's companionship. "So David, what are your plans for the future?"

"Well, I have several options. The one I am favoring is right here. I have an interest in a gardening business, as you know." Angie sensed that the two of them wished to talk in private without any interruptions.

"Excuse me," Angie interrupted, "I need to do some laundry." She stood up and hobbled to the laundry room.

"So Jennifer, what has been happening at the agency?" David asked. "I've been away for a few weeks."

"Oh, the same old stuff. Bringing down drug dealers in South America and the rest of the world. Cracking industrial spying cases and writing articles on the nation's bad guys—anywhere there is evil in the world that endangers our national security."

"So what are your plans for the future, Jennifer?" She was waiting for an entry to discuss that question and David knew it. "Any plans to settle down?"

"I'm going to be honest with you David. I want to settle down, but I need to find someone to settle down with. Work with the Agency never allowed me to circulate in the social world even

## The Garden

in my own church." David needed to weigh and speak the next few words carefully. He needed to discourage Jennifer from pursuing him with any romantic intentions. He took another sip of coffee, took a deep breath and cleared his throat.

"I want to be honest with you, if you will permit me," David responded.

"Go ahead," she stated. Jennifer knew what David was going to say to her.

"When I was a little 6th grader, I fell in love with my next door neighbor. This girl had no time for me. However, God placed upon my heart the desire to wait for her to want me. I have waited and waited and waited. All I need is for her to fall in love with me." David stopped there and waited for Jennifer to respond. She turned and looked at the open doorway down the hall into the laundry room where Angie had disappeared and wondered if she had listened to what David had just stated.

"Well," Jennifer said with a sigh, "I kind of thought that is what you would say. Let me tell you that she is crazy if she doesn't want you." Angie was able to listen to the two agents and their entire conversation through the wide open hallway. She had not started the washing machine and dryer as yet.

"I am working on it," David remarked. "I have a lot of patience. And, there is another reason I have been so diligent in keeping myself for Angie."

"What is that?" Jennifer asked. She wondered if maybe he had some financial reason for remaining unhitched during his time in the agency.

"You are one of them," he said softly. "You can't imagine how many women the agency paired me with who were beautiful, shapely, sexy, and inviting. Each time God told me to wait. Most of these women were not Christians. You were one that was. But God placed the thought in my mind: Wait for Angie — be patient."

"Well," Jennifer responded, "thank you for the compliment."

"Can you imagine what my reputation would be if I had yielded to the temptations that all these women presented?" David said honestly. "I know, and some of our agents have had to quit because of diseases they picked up in other countries — some

*The Garden*

of them sleeping with the enemy. I get your point and now I know why." Jennifer got up and prepared to leave. She had her answer as to why she came. David was not available to her even though both of them shared the same theology and goals in life.

When she finally left and David sat down and continued drinking a second cup of coffee, Angie walked through the hall door from doing some laundry.

"Did Jennifer leave?" Angie knew she left and David knew that Angie knew that she had left.

"She did. It will probably be the last time I will see her, that is, if I don't go back to the Agency."

David went out to work in the garden. Angie had much to think about. She also was at a crossroads in her life. What was she going to do next in her life? She did not have a college education, she had spent time in a rehab center on drug charges, and she never did have any career passion in her life. David wanted her but not in the spiritual condition she was currently in.

Angie finally called out, as she was sitting alone on the couch in the living room. "God do something to make me believe!"

On the next Saturday morning a terrible accident happened to Angie as she was coming out of the back door and down the steps. Her leg had healed to the point where she was able to get around without crutches. She was not fully awake and missed the last step. The fall may have not been damaging to her, but for the rock that was sitting by the two rose bushes. Her head hit the rock with enough force to place her into an unconscious state immediately. Both Helen and David were out in the garden and heard the commotion. David looked over and saw that Angie was not moving. He quickly ran over and saw that she had a cut on the side of her head. The cut was bleeding profusely. David took out his handkerchief, covered, and pressed against it firmly.

*The Garden*

"Helen, call the ambulance! Tell them to get here quickly!" David shouted. Helen ran to the phone inside their house. She called the Dalestown Emergency Service and then ran back outside.

"They are on their way—should be here within minutes." David quietly gave Angie a kiss on her head—then prayed for her, the emergency people, and the doctors that would treat her. He sensed that this injury was serious and could be life threatening. He remembered what he had told Angie when she was going through some rough times back in High school.

"Angie," David recalled saying, "someday God will land you on your back and you will call out to him. Maybe then you will finally yield to His will and believe."

The ambulance was soon at Angie's side administering first aid and preparing the stretcher for transporting her to a hospital emergency room. She did not move, indicating that she was out completely.

At the hospital emergency room they examined Angie immediately and made the decision to bring her into the MRI room. The doctors were interested in what damage had been done in the fall. As they were in the process of the MRI scan, the monitor suddenly started flashing red lights. Then, for a period of a full minute, the same monitor indicated that the heart had stopped beating. They immediately placed her on a table and began to massage her chest.

Meanwhile, David, his father and Angie's mother were in the waiting room praying passionately. The x-rays had shown that a blood clot had formed in the critical part of the brain. It would be just a matter of time and she would be gone, according to what the all three doctors were thinking. All they could do was to drain the blood out of her head. She was now in a coma.

*The Garden*

Angie was in the hospital for the next 7 days in an unconscious state. A series of machines were keeping her heart beating and providing the fluids necessary to keep her alive. The family was permitted to visit her once a day. They continued in prayer along with quietly singing gospel songs. The people of their church were engaged in around the clock prayed for her. "I am concerned for her life," David told a group of them, "but I am more concerned for her eternal spiritual condition."

A phone call woke the whole family up at 3 am on the next Sunday morning. David who was sleeping in the downstairs bedroom jumped up and ran to the phone on the dining room table. It was the hospital. "Angie just woke up," the female voice announced. "Get over here as soon as you can, she is asking for David." David woke up his dad and Helen. Then he drove over to the hospital with Ralph and Helen. When they got to the hospital David went to Angie's room. She was lying in bed wide-awake, happy and smiling.

"Angie," he said in a surprised and grateful voice, "What happened?

"David," she calmly said, "I have had an out of body experience, as they call it and as I have read in books. I was always skeptical of such occurrence, but I have had it. David, I want you to know that I am a different person. I have come over to your side of the fence, to put it in garden terms.—I was in the Canadian thistle, but now I am among the beautiful flowers." David smiled and he knew right away what had happened.

"When did it happen, Angie?"

"Just after I woke up about an hour ago," she answered. "David, I have a fantastic story to tell you. You need to hear it before I forget it. You may want to take notes because people are going to ask you and me to tell it often." David asked the attending nurse to vacate the room and asked her to hold Angie's mom and Ralph in the waiting room.

## The Garden

"I want to be alone with Angie for a short time." The nurse soon left the room and went to the waiting room to convey David's message. "Tell me Angie, what happened."

"I remember starting down the back steps. That is all I remember prior to my going into an unconscious state. I know I hit the ground with a thud! The next thing that happened, I was lifted up over this big machine and saw my body being worked on by a team of doctors. Then I was suddenly on a path with beautiful flowers on each side. I was met by a man who took my hand and led me to a place that had some stone seats. We sat down. The man was wearing a pair of blue overalls, a railroad cap and a red shirt. He had on his feet some black sandals."

"Was that person Jesus?" David asked.

"I don't know," Angie answered. "I never asked him his name. He began to talk to me."

"Angie," he said, "do you know why you are here?" I told him I did not know. "You are dead, deceased, gone from the earth." I then looked at him with a sad and scared expression.

"That can't be," I said to the man. "I have too many unresolved issues back on earth. I need to go back. I wasn't ready to go." The man looked at me for a short time, then finally said.

"Follow me." He once again took my hand and led me to a garden that was similar to Helen's and your dad's in the back yard. "Would you help David and your mother if you went back? he asked.

"Yes, I would," I responded.

"That means you would need to get your hands dirty, be on your knees, water once in a while when God doesn't send rain. When someone is in a garden of flowers, vegetables, and herbs he or she is close to God."

"Oh, I will do those things. Will I be able to come back here someday and garden?" I asked him. He looked at me with a sad expression.

"Not in your spiritual condition, he responded. Then he took me by his hand and led me back on the path with flowers on each side. Soon I was transformed and saw myself back on a table where the doctors were still working on me. Almost immediately

I was once again conscious. It took me only a split second to give myself completely to the Lord."

"The doctors came in and began examining Angie. They were all perplexed. "We cannot determine any ongoing bleeding. It's almost as if she never was injured, one of them said."

"I began to pray. Then I began to cry. The doctors started wondering what was ailing me. As I was crying, I had a vision of Jesus and he was smiling at me. I almost thought it was an extension of my out-of-body episode. So, here I am as happy and content as I'll ever be."

"Oh! One more thing—I no longer have a hatred for my father. It all vanished. I now want him to show up so I can welcome him into my home, someday."

"It's all an answer to prayer, Angie, and it answers the question of our future. Now, I will get your mom and my dad to come see you."

David informed the Agency that he was resigning. They were not happy, but were expecting it. David was retained as an advisor and would be paid per case amount which would be added to his pension amount. Some travel may be required. They would allow Angie to travel with him. He was also asked to do some writing about subjects relating to the Agency's work.

David and Angie decided to get married as soon as possible. The church where David's dad and Angie's mother attended was in a major improvement project making it impossible to hold the wedding. "Where can we have our wedding," Angie asked David as they were visiting on the two seated glider in front of the garden.

"That is a good question." David answered, with a puzzled look on his face. For the next 30 seconds they sat thinking as they stared at the garden. Suddenly, they turned to each other as though they were having the same idea.

"The garden," they both said at the same time. They then slapped their opened hands together in high fives.

"Let's start planning it right now." Angie responded. For the next hour they sat and planned their wedding. They also planned their honeymoon.

The wedding took place on August 15 and it was a sunny and warm day. Chairs from the church were brought in and set on the lawn. Several of David's former Agency partners attended—male and female, along with people from Angie's rehab center. People from the church, town, the Veggie stand customers, former high school teachers, and relatives completed the wedding guest list. David's friends from south of Dalestown whom he had helped plant their garden after getting a flat tire also came. A veggie salad was served along with wedding cake, nuts, mints, coffee, punch, and ice cream.

Their honeymoon was spent in Norway and Sweden. They began the time together by thanking the Lord for protecting them and giving them patience to wait for each other.

**The end**

CPSIA information can be obtained at www.ICGtesting.com
Printed in the USA
LVOW04s1913150815

450170LV00002B/2/P